Six-Gun Caballero

A full list of L. Ron Hubbard's
novellas and short stories is provided at the back.

*Dekalogy—a group of ten volumes

L. RON HUBBARD

SIX-GUN CABALLERO

GALAXY
PRESS

Published by
Galaxy Press, LLC
7051 Hollywood Boulevard, Suite 200
Hollywood, CA 90028

Printed in the United States of America.

ISBN-10 1-59212-299-X
ISBN-13 978-1-59212-299-8

Library of Congress Control Number 2007927531

CONTENTS

STORIES FROM PULP FICTION'S GOLDEN AGE

AND it *was* a golden age.

The 1930s and 1940s were a vibrant, seminal time for a gigantic audience of eager readers, probably the largest per capita audience of readers in American history. The magazine racks were chock-full of publications with ragged trims, garish cover art, cheap brown pulp paper, low cover prices—and the most excitement you could hold in your hands.

"Pulp" magazines, named for their rough-cut, pulpwood paper, were a vehicle for more amazing tales than Scheherazade could have told in a million and one nights. Set apart from higher-class "slick" magazines, printed on fancy glossy paper with quality artwork and superior production values, the pulps were for the "rest of us," adventure story after adventure story for people who liked to *read.* Pulp fiction authors were no-holds-barred entertainers—real storytellers. They were more interested in a thrilling plot twist, a horrific villain or a white-knuckle adventure than they were in lavish prose or convoluted metaphors.

The sheer volume of tales released during this wondrous golden age remains unmatched in any other period of literary history—hundreds of thousands of published stories in over nine hundred different magazines. Some titles lasted only an issue or two; many magazines succumbed to paper shortages during World War II, while others endured for decades yet. Pulp fiction remains as a treasure trove of stories you can read, stories you can love, stories you can remember. The stories were driven by plot and character, with grand heroes, terrible villains, beautiful damsels (often in distress), diabolical plots, amazing places, breathless romances. The readers wanted to be taken beyond the mundane, to live adventures far removed from their ordinary lives—and the pulps rarely failed to deliver.

In that regard, pulp fiction stands in the tradition of all memorable literature. For as history has shown, good stories are much more than fancy prose. William Shakespeare, Charles Dickens, Jules Verne, Alexandre Dumas—many of the greatest literary figures wrote their fiction for the readers, not simply literary colleagues and academic admirers. And writers for pulp magazines were no exception. These publications reached an audience that dwarfed the circulations of today's short story magazines. Issues of the pulps were scooped up and read by over thirty million avid readers each month.

Because pulp fiction writers were often paid no more than a cent a word, they had to become prolific or starve. They also had to write aggressively. As Richard Kyle, publisher and editor of *Argosy,* the first and most long-lived of the pulps, so pointedly explained: "The pulp magazine writers, the best of them, worked for markets that did not write for critics or attempt to satisfy timid advertisers. Not having to answer to anyone other than their readers, they wrote about human beings on the edges of the unknown, in those new lands the future would explore. They wrote for what we would become, not for what we had already been."

Some of the more lasting names that graced the pulps include H. P. Lovecraft, Edgar Rice Burroughs, Robert E. Howard, Max Brand, Louis L'Amour, Elmore Leonard, Dashiell Hammett, Raymond Chandler, Erle Stanley Gardner, John D. MacDonald, Ray Bradbury, Isaac Asimov, Robert Heinlein—and, of course, L. Ron Hubbard.

In a word, he was among the most prolific and popular writers of the era. He was also the most enduring—hence this series—and certainly among the most legendary. It all began only months after he first tried his hand at fiction, with L. Ron Hubbard tales appearing in *Thrilling Adventures, Argosy, Five-Novels Monthly, Detective Fiction Weekly, Top-Notch, Texas Ranger, War Birds, Western Stories,* even *Romantic Range*. He could write on any subject, in any genre, from jungle explorers to deep-sea divers, from G-men and gangsters, cowboys and flying aces to mountain climbers, hard-boiled detectives and spies. But he really began to shine when he turned his talent to science fiction and fantasy of which he authored nearly fifty novels or novelettes to forever change the shape of those genres.

Following in the tradition of such famed authors as Herman Melville, Mark Twain, Jack London and Ernest Hemingway, Ron Hubbard actually lived adventures that his own characters would have admired—as an ethnologist among primitive tribes, as prospector and engineer in hostile climes, as a captain of vessels on four oceans. He even wrote a series of articles for *Argosy,* called "Hell Job," in which he lived and told of the most dangerous professions a man could put his hand to.

Finally, and just for good measure, he was also an accomplished photographer, artist, filmmaker, musician and educator. But he was first and foremost a *writer,* and that's the L. Ron Hubbard we come to know through the pages of this volume.

This library of Stories from the Golden Age presents the best of L. Ron Hubbard's fiction from the heyday of storytelling, the Golden Age of the pulp magazines. In these eighty volumes, readers are treated to a full banquet of 153 stories, a kaleidoscope of tales representing every imaginable genre: science fiction, fantasy, western, mystery, thriller, horror, even romance—action of all kinds and in all places.

Because the pulps themselves were printed on such inexpensive paper with high acid content, issues were not meant to endure. As the years go by, the original issues of every pulp from *Argosy* through *Zeppelin Stories* continue crumbling into brittle, brown dust. This library preserves the L. Ron Hubbard tales from that era, presented with a distinctive look that brings back the nostalgic flavor of those times.

L. Ron Hubbard's Stories from the Golden Age has something for every taste, every reader. These tales will return you to a time when fiction was good clean entertainment and the most fun a kid could have on a rainy afternoon or the best thing an adult could enjoy after a long day at work.

Pick up a volume, and remember what reading is supposed to be all about. Remember curling up with a *great story.*

—Kevin J. Anderson

KEVIN J. ANDERSON *is the author of more than ninety critically acclaimed works of speculative fiction, including* The Saga of Seven Suns, *the continuation of the Dune Chronicles with Brian Herbert, and his* New York Times *bestselling novelization of L. Ron Hubbard's* Ai! Pedrito!

SIX-GUN CABALLERO

CHAPTER ONE

"SON," said Judge Klarner, slapping his beefy hand down upon his host's glossy linen table cloth, "I came halfway across the United States and I rode myself raw over two hundred miles of desert to keep you out of trouble. And now, damn it, you might at least listen to me!"

Michael Patrick Obañon paused in the act of helping himself to the breakfast proffered on a platter by a young Mexican. He put the silver spoon and fork back and waved the servant away.

"*Señor,*" said Michael Patrick Obañon. "Forgive me. I assure you it was only out of courtesy that I forbade you to talk until you had at least eaten. Come," he said with a flashing smile, "is it so dangerous that even breakfast must wait?"

"Dangerous!" puffed Judge Klarner. "Young man, when your daddy and mother first came to this land it was worthless. But they built! They increased their herds! They have left a heritage of a hundred thousand acres to you, their son. Have you no sense of responsibility? Can you lightly wave aside the loss of this great fortune?"

"But I did not think this was so serious. After all, the United States government will certainly recognize the old Spanish grants. And what have I to fear, my good judge?"

"What have you to fear?" roared Klarner. He left it there for a moment, to sink back with an orator's taste for dramatics. Such a question left him powerless. His great shoulders sagged inside his white broadcloth coat. Even the lodge pin on his great watch chain drooped. With a great effort he straightened out his white mustache and collected himself.

With great care, Klarner began again. "Young man, what do you suppose will happen to the overflowing scum from the California gold fields? Did you expect they would all find wealth? No! And now Gadsden has purchased all this land from Mexico. He has reserved some of it for railroad and the rest is wide open to settlement. These Americans will descend upon you like locusts!"

Michael Patrick Obañon could not restrain a smile. "*Señor,* you have been misled. You have forgotten. Perhaps I hold my title to this land from Mexico but certainly I am as good an American as any of them. I am still a citizen of the United States. How can this possibly affect me?"

That fact recalled Klarner to himself. Yes, he had forgotten. This tall, thin youngster with his blue eyes and silky black hair, with his faint Spanish accent, was indeed a citizen of the United States. Yes, he had been misled by that white silk shirt, the wide-bottomed, laced trousers, by the silvered, flat-brimmed sombrero which hung from the wall.

"I am not at all certain of your title," said Klarner, returning to the attack. "I am here as your father's friend to ask you to refile upon this land. True, you could not have your hundred thousand acres. After all, that is a nation in itself. But a few thousand can be saved before you are driven out by settlers."

4

"*Señor,*" said Michael, "my confidence in the United States would seem to be greater than yours. Certainly this is a large rancho. My father's title to it was clear enough. He was a friend of Mexico and they would not play him false. Why should I contact these lawyers you recommend just to file on what is already mine? That would imply lack of faith in my title."

Klarner lowered his great shaggy brows. "Son, the fact is this. During the last three months, the Mexican border has moved far to the south of you. Three months ago you were on Mexican soil, but now this house sits within the territorial boundaries of the United States. Any day, men will come in upon you, stake out sections of your land, drive off your cattle, deny your right to remain here. In their ignorance they will consider you a Mexican and give you scant respect as such. In memory of your parents you must take every precaution. . . ."

A *vaquero* charged through the door, pulled up to a sharp stop with a jingle of spurs and yanked off his sombrero.

"Your pardon, *don* Michael. I do not mean to interrupt your breakfast."

"What is it, Enrico?"

"*Don* Michael, some thirty men are approaching the ranch at a swift trot. They are Americanos and they are armed!"

"It looks," said Klarner, "as though I arrived too late."

"Enrico," said Michael Patrick Obañon, "how many rifles and pistols would you say our men possess?"

"Not more than ten in all including your own, *don* Michael."

"Enrico, you will withdraw those *vaqueros* in the vicinity

off to a nearby line camp and then report again to me. Oppose nothing these Americans do as we wish no one killed."

"*Sí, don* Michael. I go."

"I see, *señor el juez,* that you understand our language."

Klarner scowled. "Enough to know that I was right. You evidently intend to give up without a struggle. My boy, your father was made of sterner stuff. But Mexico City has softened his son."

Because Judge Klarner was under his roof and because the man had been his father's friend, Michael Patrick Obañon said nothing.

He beckoned for his breakfast and Antonio padded silently into the room with it.

"*Don* Michael," whispered Antonio, his brown face drawn with fear, "you will not be reckless! These men from the north and west . . . I have heard those things which have happened in California. *Don* Michael, we could not do without you. Please do not allow your reckless . . ."

"Serve the *señor,* Antonio."

"*Sí, don* Michael. I am sorry. But the people of Santa Rosa owe you . . ."

"*El juez,* Antonio."

"*Sí, don* Michael."

But Judge Klarner touched no food. His faded eyes, crouched in their webs of wrinkles, studied the calm youth before him.

Michael Patrick Obañon was a handsome fellow. He had a graceful air about him and when he spoke he made poetry with his long-fingered hands. His voice was controlled and gentle and his glance was friendly and frank. For all the world he appeared not Irish but a Castilian gentleman from the court at Madrid.

Many hoofs, dulled by the sand of the yard, came close and stopped.

Michael stood up.

"Where are you going?" demanded Klarner, staring first at Obañon and then at the silver-mounted revolver which hung holstered from a peg on the wall.

"To ask them in, of course," replied Michael, unconcerned.

Klarner caught at the leg-of-mutton silk sleeve. "Don't be a fool. We've still got time. You and I can make a run for Washington and . . ."

The door crashed inward with a swirl of dust and the two turned to face the intruder.

The man was tall and thickly built. He had a Walker pistol in his huge and horny hand and his squinted, ink-dot eyes probed the dimness of the room. His heavy, Teutonic face was almost covered by a shaggy, untrimmed beard. The faded red shirt with its big bib and pearl buttons attested that he had come from California, as did his flat-heeled miner's boots.

"Come in," said Michael with a ghost of a bow.

"Is this Santa Rosa?"

"You are correct," replied Michael. "*La hacienda de* Obañon."

The stranger turned and made a come-on gesture with his heavy Walker pistol. "This is the place, Charlie. Come on in!"

Leather creaked and voices rose.

"What the hell do I care where you eat?" roared the stranger. "There must be grub somewhere in these shacks. Go find it. You ain't helpless!"

He turned back to the room and crossed heavily to the table. A choice apple, carefully grown on the rancho, caught the stranger's eye. He picked it up, wiped it on his shirt and sank his yellow fangs into it with a loud crack. Somehow he managed to chew the bite but it impeded his speech for some little time.

Two more men appeared in the doorway.

The stranger again motioned with the pistol. "C'mon. Here's food."

One of the men was squat. His head was large and so were his features, all out of keeping with his size. Though covered with dust, his clothes were loud, consisting of a checkered vest, a yellow suit and a small green hat which he now jerked off and twisted in his hands.

"Mebbe we're intruding, Gus. Mebbe these gents ain't finished their breakfast." He took another turn on his hat and looked nervously at Michael. "Don't mind Gus. He ain't got much manners like Charlie and me."

"Think nothing of it," said Michael with another ghost of a bow, much to the amazement of Klarner. "I shall have a servant bring in more food for you."

"Hell," said Gus, gnawing on the apple, "you speak pretty good English for a damned greaser. Don't he, Mr. Lusby?"

Mr. Lusby gave his hat yet another turn and looked uncomfortable and perspiring. "You don't mind, Gus. If it's too much trouble, *señor . . .*"

"Think nothing of it," said Michael. "Please be seated."

"My name is Lusby. Julius Lusby, Mr. . . ."

"I am *don* Michael to my friends, Mr. Lusby."

"Sure. Sure. Glad to meetcha, *don* Michael. Look, this is Gus Mueller and this is Charlie Pearson."

Gus did not even bother to nod. He prowled around the big room, still gripping the Walker pistol, opening doors and closing them, bending a calculating eye upon the beautiful Indian rugs and the finely carved, imported furniture.

Charlie Pearson was leaning against the door jamb with his boots crossed. His shirt had once been white linen and his stock was flowing black silk. He had the hard but easy air of the gambler about him.

He eyed Michael suspiciously. Finally, he muttered, "Pleased," and went on picking his teeth.

"Maybe you can tell me where is the boss?" said Mr. Lusby hesitantly.

Gus came to the center of the room and tossed the apple core out the window. "Sure. We got business around here. Where's the greaser that owns this dump?"

Michael smiled. "Perhaps he has already heard of your coming."

"I get it," said Gus with a harsh laugh. "And he wasn't far from wrong, neither. I suppose you're the major-domo, huh?" And as Michael did not show any signs of doing anything but smiling politely, Gus nudged Mr. Lusby. "Show him the papers."

"Yep," said Charlie. "Show him the papers. We got to make this here thing legal."

Mr. Lusby ran his hands nervously through his pockets and at last located the documents. He edged up to the table, giving the impression of being about to run, and laid several sheets face up on the cloth.

"Since the border's moved," said Mr. Lusby, "all this is United States. I fixed it so the boys could file. And here's the deeds, all ethical and legal, to the Santa Rosa Valley. This ranch house is on it, ain't it?"

"Yes," said Michael.

"There," said Mr. Lusby with a sigh of relief. "I got it done."

Antonio came to the kitchen door and stared in.

"Hey, you," said Gus, "hustle some grub. I could eat a mule."

"*Don* Michael . . ." said Antonio.

"You heard the gentleman, Antonio."

"*Sí, don* Michael," and miserably he withdrew. A moment later came the loud crashing of dishes being thrown about.

Mr. Lusby looked apologetic. "We don't want to put you out none, *señor*. . . ."

"Naw," said Charlie. "But the point is, you'll have to find someplace to sleep. We're takin' over here."

"Naturally," said *don* Michael. "Come, judge."

"Wait a minute," said Mr. Lusby. "Look. We don't know nothing about this place. We don't know where the cows is or nothing. Maybe you want a job, huh?"

"A job?" said Michael.

"Sure," said Mr. Lusby. "You look like a pretty good feller. We'll pay you thirty dollars a month." He added hastily, "But not another nickel!"

"Why, you are too kind," said *don* Michael. "As I am out of employment, I shall be happy to accept such a liberal offer." He gave them a smile, accompanied by a floating gesture of his hands which gave them to understand that he was completely theirs to command. "And now, if you gentlemen will excuse me, I shall show your men where the forage is kept."

"That's the spirit," said Charlie unexpectedly. "When you find out the other gent's got a third ace as his hole card, don't go quittin'. Deal 'em up, I says."

Michael took his silver-encrusted sombrero from the wall and put it on, adjusting the diamond which held the flowing chin thong. He buckled the silver-inlaid pistol about his waist, and so normal did that gesture seem to the three strangers that they failed to note it.

Michael motioned to Judge Klarner and walked out into the hot morning sunlight of the yard.

CHAPTER TWO

DON MICHAEL stopped on the edge of a rose garden, transfixed by the havoc which was being wreaked upon the rancho by the twenty-seven. In a few seconds the tenseness went out of his shoulders and he lounged against the side of the arched gate, studiously building himself a cigarette.

Klarner stared at him with squinted, puzzled eyes. Tim Obañon, when Klarner had known him twenty-eight years before, had been a wild Irish gentleman with an uncontrollable temper. He had finally almost outlawed himself from diplomatic circles in Washington and had gone to Mexico, where his personality and fame had been rewarded with this great grant of land.

But Michael Patrick Obañon, born in Mexico and never out of it in his life until the border had shifted under his feet, was certainly not old Tim. The beautiful clothes, the perfect manners and poise, the Latin gestures . . .

"Aren't you going to *do* anything?" roared Klarner. "Are you going to let them slap you without retaliation? Get your money from your bank and we'll rush to Washington and fight this. You can still file. . . ."

"Money?" smiled *don* Michael. "I have land, cattle, a people,

13

I have saddles and buildings and more cattle—more than I can ever count. But of the actual specie, my good judge, I have not more than five pesos."

"Then you're licked," growled Klarner. "Your father would have foreseen this. He wrote and asked me to watch out for you, but I was detained. If I had only gotten here sooner!"

"But you did not," said Michael.

Bleakly he looked at the scene before him. *La hacienda de Obañon* proper consisted of half a hundred 'dobe buildings built in the orderly fashion of a town. There was a blacksmith shop, a *tienda* where one could buy *frijoles* and tobacco, a church without a steeple but a church just the same, a cock-fight ring, forage storehouses, *charqui* shelters, as well as many cleanly whitened huts of varying sizes depending upon the position of the *vaquero* and the numerousness of his *familia*.

Klarner was astonished at the result of *don* Michael's quiet order. The *vaqueros* had indeed withdrawn, taking with them their families and as much baggage as could be packed in ten minutes. A fire still smoldered in the forge of the blacksmith shop and the dust had scarcely settled in the corrals.

One lone inhabitant remained behind, a Franciscan father, who stood on the steps of his church, hands in his sleeves, his sober face a study in quietness.

But the *padre* was the only quiet person in *la hacienda de Obañon*. Twenty-seven men filled the place with shouts and swirling dust, crossing and recrossing the narrow, sun-baked street, hailing each other with trophies lifted high.

They were conducting themselves more like *filibusteros*

than homesteaders and they had the air of having taken the place after much effort, thereby earning the privilege to loot.

A cradle sailed out of a doorway to land with a splintering crash, followed by a coffee pot which in turn was dented by a lead crucifix. The street was filling up with cast away bedding and clothes, cooking pots, furniture, saddles, sombreros, pictures, broken dishes and bright Indian rugs.

Above the growing din, Klarner said, "They won't leave much of this place, son. You had better come to Washington. You can file on a few acres and salvage . . ."

Don Michael smiled and shrugged, "My good judge, I appreciate your efforts on my behalf. But I am afraid it wouldn't be the sporting thing."

"But good heavens, young fellow, you can't fight without guns. These men are trained toughs, the sweepings of the Barbary Coast and the gold camps. They are the worst possible element of society. There is not one of these men unwanted by the law in the States. Unfortunately, the money required to obtain a decision or even to buy guns and hire fighters is not in your possession. Alone, you will be killed the instant you raise your hand and voice against them."

"Señor," drawled *don* Michael, "you draw a most unhappy picture of this. But what of my *vaqueros*? This is their home. And there are a hundred thousand acres in Santa Rosa Valley. Across this vast region are many other villages. The people, rightly or wrongly, look to me for some protection against such things. Some years ago, when the Apaches came, the government of Mexico sent me troops and we drove the Indians

back. But then the troops were recalled because of the war and now this is no longer Mexico. But I cannot believe, my good judge, that the government of the United States intends to wrong anyone."

"Government is collective," said Klarner. "It does not think. Yes, there is a Federal judge moving into Los Diablitos a day's ride north. But he can do nothing against these filed claims."

"A Federal judge?"

"Certainly. The United States is establishing territorial rule."

"Two hundred miles to the north," said *don* Michael, "also runs the telegraph. Three hundred miles to the south is the Mexican town of Carmen. . . ."

He stopped and looked up. The priest was approaching, walking with a firm step without any attempt to avoid the bedlam in the street, without replying to any of the shouts hurled at him.

"*Don* Michael," said the *padre*, "is it to be countenanced that they ruin our people?"

"I am sorry, father," said *don* Michael.

"By what law do they do this, *don* Michael."

"By a very blind law, *padre* Ramon."

"Then this is the end of *la hacienda de* Obañon, my son?"

"*Padre* Ramon, you have often said that the only ending is the last act."

"I am glad of this, *don* Michael. These swine, however, are armed and trained to fight. Must we sacrifice our poor people at the muzzle of their guns?"

"I had not thought so, father."

"Good, *don* Michael. Then only your wits intervene between this rapacity and what has been a paradise."

"*Padre* Ramon," said *don* Michael, "there is a favor which you can do for me."

"Certainly, my son."

"You know the place to which the *vaqueros* have gone. Enrico there awaits further orders. Tell him this: For one week secretly collect all stock at this end of the valley and drive it south. This Saturday I shall meet my men at the place where they are now."

"Perhaps these outlaws will object to this taking of stock, *don* Michael."

"With enough outriders, enough quiet, the thing can be done."

"It is dangerous. It is more dangerous for you to remain here."

"They have employed me, *padre* Ramon."

A faint smile greeted the reckless grin of *don* Michael.

"Then they cannot know who you are, my son."

"They do not."

"And if they discover it they will kill you. This is too dangerous!"

"My favor, *padre* Ramon."

"I go, my son."

Klarner watched him stride back through the noisy street. "I don't know what you're up to, Michael, but it looks crazy to me. I say run while you're still alive."

"That," said *don* Michael, carefully dusting his white cuff, "would take out all the fun."

"Fun?"

"Fun," said *don* Michael.

CHAPTER THREE

FOR a week everyone had been very busy. Charlie Pearson had ridden far and wide, his mathematical mind tabulating everything in sight. Gus Mueller had lumbered about the rancho keeping the men at their tasks of getting settled and used to their immediate business. From dawn until midnight, Julius Lusby hunched over his papers, his nose so close to the sheet that the pen occasionally touched it, leaving ink smears he neglected to wash off.

Lusby's inventory was very complete. He had not overlooked so much as a rivet in the harness shop. He was not sure just why he was so accurate about it, but business to Lusby was business.

It was Saturday, mid-afternoon, and he was still working on his records, perspiring until he was forced to unbutton his checkered vest.

Gus was sprawled at length upon the silken couch, his spurs leaving small perforations in a beautiful brocaded cushion. He was chewing a raw carrot, which novelty he had discovered in the great gardens behind the rambling ranch house.

Charlie, powdered with dust, quirt dangling from his wrist, watchful eyes restless, came quietly into the room. Lusby did not hear him come up to the carved hardwood desk and, seeing him suddenly, gave a leaping start.

"Oh. It's you," said Lusby, patting his face with a red handkerchief.

"Yeah," said Charlie. "It's me. The cards are all dealt and if somebody don't ring in no holdout we're going to scoop up the blue chips. When do we begin the drive north?"

"Aw, hold on your pants," said Gus. "I've had enough of riding to last me a while. What's the hurry?" He wrapped his fingers around the neck of a wine bottle and chased the carrot with Madeira.

"I got a hunch," said Charlie.

"You got a hunch?" said Lusby, frightened.

"Yep, I got a hunch. And you know me when I get a hunch. Somebody's got four kings in their pants' cuff. I says, let's grab up what cattle is in sight and drive north to the railroad. We'll ship them and then if anything happens to show we have title to land and not cattle too, we still got blue chips to cash in."

"Aw, you always was an old woman. You'd shy at a sagebrush," snorted Gus.

"One of these days," said Charlie, "you're going to bluff that hand too far, Gus."

"I'm scared to death. I'm shakin' in my boots. G'wan, what's the matter with you? We got the title—or leastways *you* two have. . . ."

"We got the tickets," said Charlie. "And if you want to get funny, you're going to get left out in the rain. As far as a say in this round goes, you don't hold a pair of deuces, understand? Keep your mouth shut or I'll shut it for you."

"You'd cut me off?" yelled Gus, leaping up, hand stabbing to his big Walker pistol.

Charlie's hand shot inside his frock coat, but Lusby was immediately up and between them. "Now, boys. Nerves it is, that's all. Just nerves. You got to stop this fightin', boys. Sure, I put up the money, didn't I? And Charlie put up the brains. And we don't leave nobody out if he don't go monkeying around the cash drawer, do we, Charlie?"

Gus caught Lusby by the coat and whipped him aside. "Listen, you shriveled up tin-pan peddler, maybe you put up the money, but who hired the men, huh? Who saw you through?"

"Please," whimpered Lusby, patently frightened of Gus. "I don't mean no harm. You can have a share more than you was going to get. You . . ."

"The devil he can!" snapped Charlie. "He saw his cards when they was dealt and he didn't squawk then. Let go of Julius, you bag of breeze."

Gus met Charlie's stare but only for an instant. Like a cur pup Gus shifted his gaze unwillingly to the floor. His face was flushed and his eyes were red.

"Sit down on that couch," said the lean, hard Charlie.

Gus sat down.

"You get your pay and that's all," added Charlie. "There ain't enough in this pot for it to be cut three ways."

"Maybe he's right," shivered Lusby. "Maybe we ought to give him . . ."

"We give him nothin'!" snapped Charlie. "We been through

this before and I'm sick of it. I'm so sick of Mueller . . . Let it go. I came in here to tell you that I wanted all the stock brought up for shipment."

"Sure," said Lusby. "But ain't you got it all up now?"

"Me?" said Charlie. "I ain't had nothin' to do with that. I looked it over early in the week and we can get three thousand head within ten miles of this ranch, taking nothing but the best. You was supposed to roll them in, Mueller. Where did you and the boys work them?"

"Three thousand head?" said Gus. "You're crazy. We combed the gullies right around here yesterday and we couldn't find more than a dozen good beeves."

"If you're lying to me . . ." began Charlie. "Look, I've been riding day and night over this whole country, trying to find out just how many cattle there are on this range. I *know* there were three thousand within ten miles of here. Mueller, if you're covering up and trying your hand on the side . . ."

"I tell you," shouted Gus, "that the whole bunch of us only combed up a dozen. We thought they'd be someplace else on the place, see? We . . ."

"Something is wrong," said Lusby.

"I knew it! I told you I had a hunch!" Charlie faced Lusby. "It's that greaser. He's got a holdout sure as hell. And where's Obañon, the guy that was supposed to own all this. If he ain't him I'll eat that fancy hat of his!"

"Now, now," said Lusby. "Don't get excited, Charlie. That Spanish boy is the politest gent I ever met. And he's too young for a big outfit like this. Why, he ain't more than twenty-six or so and when I was his age I didn't have more than two packs of cooking pans and assorted buttons and . . ."

"We've heard all about that before," snapped Charlie. "I tell you he's the holdout, the extra ace in the deck. . . ."

"*Señores,*" said *don* Michael, leaning against the door casing and languidly fanning himself with his sombrero, "if I intrude I am sorry."

"No, no," said Mr. Lusby. "Come on in. This . . . we're just having a argument, that's all. A little, friendly argument, huh, boys?"

Charlie glared.

"But I do not wish to interrupt," said *don* Michael. "The house, after all, is yours."

"Look here, spiggoty," grated Charlie. "Monday there was three thousand good beeves within two hours of this ranch. They're gone. What's the hole card?"

"The hole card?" said *don* Michael. "I do not understand."

Charlie almost burst his buttons. But he kept his voice level. "What's happened to those cattle? I saw them with my own eyes!"

"The cattle?" said *don* Michael. "Ah, now I know what you mean. Why, *señor,* at this time of year the water grows less and the cattle drift south. They sometimes move in a matter of days."

"Sure," said Lusby. "Now you *see,* Charlie?"

"*Señores,*" said *don* Michael, "if there is anything I can do to help, do not fail to state it. I am desolated that the rancho should give you trouble. My . . ."

23

"Look here," said Charlie. "What happened to this Obañon? He didn't just vanish in smoke."

"Of course not," replied *don* Michael, with a small shrug. "But he valued his life and he took the course of least danger, naturally."

"There's another joker in this deck," snarled Charlie. "Obañon better not let me catch up with him, *whoever he is.* If I thought he was causing this beef to be shuffled . . ."

"Please," begged Lusby. "Don't talk like that before this gentleman. Maybe you want something, *don* Michael?"

"Why, yes. I came to request that you allow me to visit a poor *peón* tonight. The word has come that he is to name his child after me and I must go, of course."

"Sure!" said Lusby. "That's a good one! Maybe," he added with a gross wink intended to be sly, "maybe he's got plenty of reason, seein' you're the handsome feller you are."

Michael smiled politely. "Thank you, *señor* Lusby. It is a privilege to work for such a courteous gentleman." He bowed and swept his hat back upon his head and strolled away, silver spurs making music as he walked.

"You hear that?" grinned Lusby. "He said it was a privilege. . . ."

"Bah!" said Charlie with an emphatic scowl. "You've got the light in your eyes. You're hypnotized by his fancy manners and his clothes. You'd lick the boots of anybody that told you you were good. Mueller, get the boys."

"Why?" said Gus, sitting where he was as an angry gesture.

"Do I have to tell you everything?" cried Charlie. "Why

in the name of God I had to get a puffed-up fool and a thick-witted Dutchman in on my deal I don't know! Damn you, get those men! As soon as that goddamned greaser rides away we're going to follow. He's bound to lead us to that missing beef!"

CHAPTER FOUR

T HE night was sharp and brittle-black, lighted only by uncounted diamond stars which gave inky outline to the ragged, gigantic mountains which rimmed the plain.

Cactus and sagebrush and boulders stood upon the approach of the two horsemen to give form to the trail which seemed to end always twenty feet in front.

It was the kind of a night which makes a man feel a hundred feet tall and capable of throwing a longhorn steer a mile and a half. The pace of the horses was brisk and they shook their heads and snorted just to hear their curb bits make jingling and exciting music.

Even Judge Klarner, an immense bulk of white when contrasted to the slim grace of his companion, felt some of the exhilaration. But Judge Klarner was as pessimistic as he was gruff and big and he expressed his emotion in his own peculiar way.

"So you think you can make a fight for it. So you think you, one man whose brain-training for war has been strumming a guitar, can stand up against that whole pack of killers. It is a gesture. You do not even intend to go through with it. You'll stick with it as long as you find it amusing and then you'll cut and run. Bah! If Tim Obañon were here, he would do this thing differently!"

"He," said *don* Michael softly, "is not here."

"You might do well to wish he were. He'd get a dozen cases of rifles down here and kill these renegades off to a man!"

"And lose half a hundred *vaqueros*, honest men with families, in the process. But pardon, *señor el juez*. I regret my ability to displease you with my methods. I am downcast to think that I can never measure up to the glorious example of my father. He was indeed a fighting man, trained for war. But I, *señor el juez*, know only the steps of the *baile*, the names of the *matadores*, the love songs with which to amuse *las señoritas*. *Señor el juez*, if you could but point a better way. . . ."

Klarner looked closely through the dark to see if *don* Michael made fun of him. But he saw no flash of white teeth.

"Well," blustered Klarner, "if I were doing it, I'd quit this nonsense of moving cattle out of reach for no other purpose than to give your *vaqueros* exercise. I tell you, you cannot last! With money, perhaps, you could fight this case and win back some of this land. But here you sit playing your foolish game because it is 'fun' while these renegades strip you of everything. In Washington . . ."

"Hush," said *don* Michael so urgently that Klarner felt the hair stand up on the back of his neck.

"You heard something?" whispered the judge, stopping.

Don Michael had reined in. He turned in his saddle and looked back. The cold night wind rippled the white silk of his shirt and tinkled the silver of his bolero.

From afar came the repeated sound. A horse had rolled a rock underfoot. Another mount was heard to trot sharply down the bank of an arroyo.

Don Michael faced front. Not far distant gleamed three squares of yellow, bright in this clear air, indicating the spot where Enrico and the men waited.

"*Señor,*" said *don* Michael. "At least a dozen men are following us. Unhappily, the *vaqueros* cannot be warned in time. But they have extra horses."

"What do you mean?"

"Softly, *señor el juez.* Please, if I request one small favor of you to save the lives of my good men, would you grant it?"

"Why . . . why . . . yes, certainly."

"Then please dismount, my good judge, and run with all silence and all speed to those huts in the distance and tell them to remove themselves and their families again to the south, to Campo Resinaldo. You can remember that?"

"What . . . what do you intend to do?"

"The lack of a rider will not be noticed. I shall lead your horse with me and turn here on this other trail, toward the place where the cattle are being held. Quickly, *señor.*"

"But why lead them to the cattle?"

"These steers are wild. They stampede easily. Go, man, before it is too late!"

The judge slid out of his saddle and lumbered at a trot ahead and out of sight.

Don Michael took his bridle and led the mount at a leisurely pace in a direction at right angles to the lights. Behind him more stones rolled. He knew, did *don* Michael, that white silk is visible at a great distance even upon the darkest of nights.

For a full hour he continued upon his way, with the star clock slowly turning about the Pole Star in the brilliant sky.

The rocks continued to roll at intervals, drawing further back now that the country was opening up.

A cigarette was glowing in the bushes beside the trail. It dropped and vanished.

"*Don* Michael," said a sibilant voice.

"Jorge, my good fellow. How goes it with the herd?"

"Excellent, *don* Michael. We have cleared the country all about the rancho. We did not know that many cattle were there, so close. We thought most of them were . . ."

"Pardon, Jorge, but there are certain things which cannot wait. Swiftly, my little one, go around the herd and pick up all the guards as you go. Take them to the west and should you hear firing, yell and dash in among the cattle and stampede them away from here."

"You have someone behind you, *don* Michael! I hear . . ."

"Yes. Of course, Jorge. Lead this horse with you and do not lose him. *Señor el juez* has admired its saddle and we cannot lose it before we present it to him. Swiftly, my brave one. And with silence."

Jorge was gone.

Don Michael crooked his supple leg about the solid silver horn of his saddle and casually built himself a cigarette, mostly by the sense of touch.

Before him came the horn-against-horn click of a large herd, the stamping of hoofs and occasional lowing sharpened by the brisk air.

Behind him there was a smooth, flat rock in the trail and across it came fourteen sets of iron shoes by the count. The line of riders could now be seen against the stars.

Before him came the horn-against-horn click of a large herd,
the stamping of hoofs and occasional lowing sharpened
by the brisk air.

Don Michael put the unlighted cigarette into his mouth and silently turned his horse. He drew out his revolver.

Abruptly he jabbed his horse with both sharp spurs. The animal lunged forward with a squeal of amazement, blindly rushing up the inclined trail.

Michael fired into the air, riding low over his horn, hat pinned back by the wind.

Ahead loomed a horseman, startled into immobility for a fatal instant. *Don* Michael crashed into him.

Instinctively the other rider grabbed for his assailant and clutching fingers found the streaming end of *don* Michael's neckerchief. With a jerk which almost hung him, *don* Michael felt the silk rip in two.

Panic threw the others hastily from the trail. Six-guns smashed out an untimed cannonade.

From afar came wild, ululating shouts as the *vaqueros* started the herd in motion and the thunder of longhorn hoofs made the earth quake.

For a space of minutes bedlam reined and then all was quiet again. Dust was mingling with white powder smoke and the departing herd was only a far-off mutter of hoofs.

CHAPTER FIVE

DON MICHAEL streaked into the darkened street of *la hacienda de* Obañon and pulled to a rearing halt before he came close to the quarters where the remainder of the *renegados* were quartered. With feverish swiftness he uncinched and jerked saddle and bridle from his mount to send the animal away with a sharp slap on the rump.

Skirting the huts he came upon the main ranch house from the side, pausing only long enough to toss his equipment into a shed.

He rushed into the front room and applied match to candles and then, still hurrying, dashed into his bedroom and stripped off his lather-stained shirt and pants and boots to replace them with cool, clean clothing. The segment of neckerchief caused him some concern and he stood undecided in the center of the floor for an instant, holding it.

Outside he heard a number of horses coming.

Hurriedly he stuffed the scrap of silk into his pocket and hurried into the front room. His fingers flew as he built himself a cigarette. He stabbed it at a candle and lighted it, throwing himself forcefully back into an easy chair.

Boots grated and spurs jingled on the porch. The door banged inward, forced open by a rider backing up.

Two of them were carrying Gus with solemn concern. Lusby was worried and unable to stand still. Charlie alone appeared unaffected. They bore Gus to the couch and laid him upon it to turn and stare stupidly at *don* Michael.

The young Irish gentleman yawned elaborately and stretched out his boots. "Ah, *señores*, your pardon. But I was asleep. *Ai*, what is this? Was he thrown from his horse?"

The group watched him get up.

Charlie's face contracted savagely, his hand blurred and a Derringer snapped out of his sleeve into his palm. "Stay put, spiggoty. We won't take any bottom deal from a man and let him live. There was five aces in this pack and we know it was you that slipped in the extra ticket. Back up against that wall and hoist your grubhooks. Quick!"

Don Michael looked in polite astonishment at the Derringer. "*Don* Charlie, you startle me. What has occurred? If there is anything I have done, I am very sorry."

"Leave him alone, Charlie," said Lusby, bending over Gus and feeling for a pulse. "Ain't you able to tell a gentleman when you see one?"

"Back up!" said Charlie.

"*Señor*, I assure you there has been some mistake," said *don* Michael. "I am utterly unable to connect any action of mine with the *señor* Mueller's falling from his horse."

"Spiggoty," said Charlie, "you know goddamned well that Gus Mueller didn't fall off no horse. He was plugged in the back and you're the gent that done it. Where's your six-gun?"

Don Michael looked bewildered. "You mean *señor* Mueller

34

has been attacked?" He moved toward the couch. "Perhaps there is something which I can do. . . ."

"No," said Lusby, dropping the horny hand back to the couch. "There ain't anything you can do. He's dead."

"Where's your gun?" said the single-track Charlie.

"Of course," said *don* Michael. "A moment please. It is in my room."

Charlie followed him to the door and watched while *don* Michael pulled the other pistol of his silver-inlaid brace down from his closet wall. Holding the weapon to Charlie by the cartridge belt, *don* Michael smiled apologetically.

"I am so sorry to cause you concern. If there is anything I can do, speak by all means."

Charlie herded *don* Michael back into the front room. Carefully, then, Charlie examined the loads of the six-gun and sniffed at the barrel. Mystified he stared at Lusby.

"It ain't been shot in a week and it ain't been cleaned neither."

"You see?" said *don* Michael.

"I told you he was a gentleman, Charlie. There's something rotten."

"To hell with the gun. It don't make no difference. We tracked this greaser and then all hell broke loose. All right. He must have done it! Where's that piece of silk Gus was holding in his hand?"

One of the men produced it and handed it over. Charlie waved it insolently before *don* Michael's nose. "You see this? Well . . ."

The door swung inward again and Judge Klarner stood

blinking in the light of the many candles. He was in deplorable condition. His face was scratched and his clothing was torn from his long run through the cactus and sage. As he had grown overheated he had pulled his silken stock from his throat and opened his shirt.

"What's the matter?" said Klarner, staring at Gus.

"Where you been?" demanded Charlie.

"Why . . . er . . . ah . . . I've . . . er . . . been out for a ride."

"With this greaser?" said Charlie.

"Certainly not!" cried the judge.

"Were you with him when he killed Mueller?"

"Is Mueller dead?" said Klarner, bushy brows lowered.

"*Señor el juez,*" said *don* Michael, "what is the meaning of this? Why are you in such ragged condition? Certainly the ride you took with one of the *vaqueros* could not have done all this to you."

"What's this about a ride with a *vaquero*?" cried Charlie, staring at Klarner.

"I know nothing about it," said *don* Michael, "except that the judge went out with a man who came here for him earlier in the evening."

Charlie whirled on *don* Michael. "Where were you?"

"I?" said *don* Michael. "Why, *señor*, it was but a step to the christening and I walked."

"There's something to that," said Lusby. "Maybe we followed the wrong man, Charlie."

Suspiciously, Charlie looked from *don* Michael back to Klarner, juggling the Derringer in his long-fingered hand.

He remembered the silk he held and looked down at it. "You seen this before, Klarner?"

The judge looked at it and scowled. "Certainly not!"

Don Michael was astounded. "What? Why, *señor el juez,* don't you recognize your own neckerchief?"

Swiftly *don* Michael crossed the room to the judge and before that worthy knew what was happening, *don* Michael had reached into his pockets, pulling a torn fragment of silk out of the last.

Swiftly, *don* Michael held it close to Charlie's piece. Of course, they matched perfectly.

"Ah, *señor el juez,*" said *don* Michael, sadly. "To think that you would so illy use my faith in you. To think that you would actually murder one of my honest employers. To think . . . !"

"He done it!" shouted Lusby, grabbing Gus' Walker pistol and leveling it at the judge.

"My God!" shouted Klarner. "What the hell is this all about? I haven't killed anyone. I didn't have a neckerchief like that! I don't know anything. . . ."

"Shut up!" snapped Charlie. "I ain't no ways convinced but we seem to have you dead to rights with an extra deck in your pants. And as for you, spiggoty, watch your step."

"It's murder he done," said Lusby, red with anger as he faced Klarner. "We'll fix you, mister. There's a Federal judge at Diablitos and he'll take care of you. We got to have law and order, that's what we got to have. Come on, Charlie. Get some of the boys. We'll send this here killer on his way tonight."

Unwillingly, Charlie tore his stare away from *don* Michael.

He looked back at the tall Irishman twice before he reached the door.

Klarner was sputtering and protesting, shouting and puffing, condemning *don* Michael and begging him for help in the same breath.

Don Michael shrugged a Latin shrug and sat down, casually beginning to roll himself a careful cigarette.

Charlie was back in a few minutes and the waiting guard could be heard gathering outside.

"Give me some dough, Julius," said Charlie. "If I can, I'll bring back the boys I sent for."

Julius Lusby turned over the prisoner to two riders and Klarner was dragged away, spluttering. Lusby got out a strong box and peeled off some bills as though he handled the most delicate lace.

"Now don't go gettin' in no games, Charlie. We're short on cash."

"We'll have plenty of cash if I bring the big crew back. I'll make arrangements for trailing about ten thousand head of beef while I'm at it."

"Sure," said Lusby, pleased at the thought of it. "You think we can get this pretty soon?"

"In about twelve days we ought to have the herd ready to drive with more help. And unless," said Charlie, giving *don* Michael a hard look, "unless a couple jokers pop into the deal, everything will be set. Listen, I'm going to tell the judge that we're giving these greasers until Monday after next to clear out and give us free use of this land."

"Sure. That makes it legal," said Lusby. "You got good brains, Charlie."

"Yeah," said Charlie, "we can't all have money."

He stalked out and closed the door behind him.

Don Michael watched blue smoke languidly rolling up toward the lofty ceiling.

CHAPTER SIX

ON a high bleak knoll was the cemetery of *la hacienda de Obañon*. The wind bowed the tall brown grasses upon it and moaned in the scraggly branches of the dead pine which stood alone against the evening sky.

A new mound of earth was red and raw and above it stood the crossed arms to mark the grave of Gus Mueller.

A long and curving path connected the crest with the rancho and through the overgrown weeds a man toiled upward, the wind pinning back the brown robe against his legs.

At the top, *padre* Ramon stopped. He was breathing hard after his long climb and he waited until he had rested before he approached the grave.

He stopped with the tips of his sandals pressing into the edge of the red earth and for many minutes he did not move.

At last he lifted his head, staring out across the twilight plains to the jagged mountains in the crystal distance over which the sun was painting a vast and turbulent canvas all in scarlet, an aweing, gargantuan display of vivid color.

"It will take many prayers," said a voice behind him, "to ease that fellow on his journey."

Padre Ramon turned. "*Don* Michael."

He was sitting upon a ledge of rock, one small, silver-spurred

41

boot perched high and the other swinging free. He smiled as he rolled a cigarette.

"What are you doing here, my son?"

"*Padre,* I think so much of our rancho that I even take pity upon the stomachs of the buzzards. I supervised his burial."

"You jest, my son. But I fear you would jest into the teeth of the devil."

"Have you seen Enrico?"

"Yes, *don* Michael. He is very much upset. Patrols of these *renegados* ride daily across the range. It is only a matter of time until they will drive our poor people from the land and thrust them destitute into *Mejico.* Enrico is much concerned with the length of time it is taking for the arrival of certain boxes to which he attaches great importance."

"Rifles and powder and bullets, father."

"Then you will fight!"

Don Michael let the smoke dribble slowly from his thin, delicate nostrils. "What else can we do? Certainly we must fight. But we cannot unless those arms arrive in time. It is a long way for them to come and we have such a little while."

"I pray that they come in time, my son. These patrols destroy everything before them, run off the cattle and bring them north and have several times shot at our *vaqueros.* With our hundreds armed, these twenty-seven bravos will find little leisure."

"Such sentiments for a priest," smiled *don* Michael.

"*Ai,* sentiments perhaps better fitted to a soldier. But I have raised our people. I have christened them and married them. I cannot see them destroyed by the avarice of a few outlaws. When will these guns come?"

Don Michael shrugged. "If they are not here very shortly, we will meet them in Mexico—or at least you people will meet them."

"You seem melancholy. Is it possible that you would remain behind at the mercy of these beasts?"

"Where honor is concerned, father, strange things are done. But think nothing of that."

"*Don* Michael, do not worry about these guns. This handful of men will take a long while to comb a hundred thousand acres. There is chance for much delay. . . ."

"Is there?" said *don* Michael with a bitter smile. He extended his hand toward the north.

Padre Ramon turned slowly and stared.

A line like a snake was coming at a crawling pace, twisted over the rough land. Though it was far away and the light dim, dots of brilliance glittered along the cavalcade. There were something more than a hundred horsemen, riding in the slipshod fashion of individual fighters, cocksure and as hard of body as they were of eye.

Padre Ramon faced *don* Michael. "But these . . . It is impossible! There will be no chance to stand against those men whether or not the guns arrive. My son, this is suicide! In a matter of days they will sweep all cattle from the range. And then they will turn upon us and murder us! You must get our people together and escape while there is yet time!"

Don Michael dropped his cigarette to earth and ground it under his heel.

"No, *padre*. Upon the flip of a coin depends success or failure. I shall wait to see where and how that coin lands."

CHAPTER SEVEN

FOUR days later, Michael Patrick Obañon rode into Diablitos alone. It was early afternoon and the weathered, weary town suffered under the broiling sun, completely inert. The 'dobe houses, which had been the entire settlement under Mexican rule, had been supplemented by new, crude construction and two stiff rows of army tents, at the head of which floated the Stars and Stripes.

Don Michael looked the place over with some amusement. It had been called Diablitos by the *vaqueros* because here they could assemble and drink *pulque* and strum their guitars and generally submit to the mild course of vice. But all mildness appeared to have departed. There were three new saloons and only one restaurant. On the verandas lounged a strange, lean breed, newly emigrated from the north—men with guns at their hips and the same steel polish to their eyeballs.

The old building which had housed the *calabozo* was now partly given over, according to a modest sign, to the Federal court. Military law prevailed, as exemplified by a sleepy, sweating trooper who leaned upon his cavalry carbine outside the door.

Don Michael dismounted and the trooper came to life. The sight of a silver sombrero, silver conchas on a saddle, and a tall, black-haired, blue-eyed youth was too uncommon to be missed. When *don* Michael started up the steps the trooper straightened his blue jacket and stood at attention.

"I wish to see the Federal judge," said *don* Michael.

"Inside," said the trooper.

Judge Summers dozed in a swivel chair, eyeglasses drooping on his long red nose. He came to life at the sound of jingling spurs and looked up to behold *don* Michael.

"*Señor,*" said *don* Michael, "I have come to see my friend, Judge Klarner, if I may be honored by your permission."

"Certainly. Certainly. Sad case."

"He is coming to trial soon?"

"In about a week. No two ways about it. The man's guilty."

"I thought," said *don* Michael with a smile, "that he had yet to be tried."

"A mere preliminary to the hanging," said Judge Summers. "I have already reviewed all evidence."

"Except this," said *don* Michael presenting an envelope well garnished with big seals. "However, I must ask you not to open it until the day of the trial. I may not be able to appear at that time."

"Evidence?"

"Yes," said *don* Michael, "of a very startling nature."

"Thank you," said Judge Summers.

"He is to be tried, then, next Monday?"

"Yes. Next Monday, just a week away." Summers yelled for a soldier.

Don Michael was escorted down the 'dobe corridor to the dim cells at the rear of the building and as he passed a few luckless felons stared in wonder at him. But not Klarner.

Klarner was up and gripping the bars so hard that they appeared in danger of crumbling in his hands.

"So you've got the brass to come here, have you?" roared Klarner.

"*Señor el juez,*" smiled *don* Michael when the guard had gone, "you excite yourself unduly. I am sad beyond description that you must languish here for sixteen days. It is, I know, so very hot."

"Not half as hot as I'd like to make it for you, you young traitor! You've framed me!"

"Of course," said *don* Michael. "How could it be otherwise?"

"How could . . . ? Why, damn your soul! If I ever get out of this alive I'll shoot you on sight! To think that I came halfway across the continent and rode through two hundred miles of desert to be accused of murder by the son of my best friend! To think I was actually trying to help you!"

"You are helping me, *señor el juez.*"

"But, dammit, there's a limit! You are doing nothing to help yourself or to help me. You've got a harebrained scheme which didn't work and now you'll let me hang for you! You're a young, empty-headed fool!"

"Ah, now," said *don* Michael, "that is very strong. I regret the necessity of having placed you here, but you will admit that my *vaqueros* have faith in me, not in you. It is I who must remain free. At least for the moment."

"Damn your *vaqueros*!" And then Klarner paused and looked puzzled. "What do you mean, free for a little while."

"There is just a chance, *señor el juez,* that you malign me. I doubt that I would suffer you to hang for me."

47

"You mean you've done something about it? You've confessed?"

Slowly, *don* Michael rolled a cigarette and carefully lighted it with a flaring phosphorous match. "In the hands of the Federal judge is an envelope which will explain everything. Your social position is strong enough that you will be released, perhaps, on the strength of that envelope." He took a slow drag at his cigarette and grinned as the smoke dribbled from his thin nostrils.

"Then . . . then you'll give yourself up?"

Don Michael shrugged. "Unless something happens, you will be hanged, no?"

"Dammit, yes! *What did you say* in that envelope?"

"*Señor el juez,* I signed, sealed and had witnessed a statement to the effect that I take the full responsibility for the death of Gus Mueller."

Incredulity flooded the judge's face. "But . . . but that means they'll hang *you* for it!"

Don Michael shrugged again and turned to go.

"Damn you, I don't believe it!" cried the judge. "I don't. . . ."

But *don* Michael was already turning the corner of the hall.

He gathered up his reins and walked, leading his mount, toward the headquarters tent of the cavalry troops.

Horses dozed in their corrals, sleepily switching at flies. The sides of the tents were lifted and here and there a trooper's feet protruded from the end of his cot. It was a peaceful scene.

Don Michael stopped before the biggest tent and looked in. At his field desk a bored company clerk wrote at the rate of a word an hour.

On a canvas chair at the back of the tent the captain dozed, his mouth wide open, his blouse collar undone, one boot half off and giving the appearance of a broken leg.

"Pardon," said *don* Michael.

The captain sat up straight and scrubbed his red face to wake himself. Then he blinked, blinded by the sun on silver.

"Pardon, *señor el capitán*," said the Irish gentleman. "I perhaps should have first found your orderly."

Captain Greyfuss fumbled to get his collar fastened. He jerked on his boot and stood up. He was not very pleased to be so caught by such an obviously personable gentleman.

"Come in!" boomed Greyfuss. "Goddammit, Byles, take the gentleman's horse!"

Byles, the clerk, though it was not his duty, was shot out of the tent by the captain's tone.

Don Michael loosened his chin thong by pulling down the silver clasp and removed his flat sombrero.

The big, red-faced captain shook his hand. "Dammit, there's been nothing but drunks here in so long. . . . Not a drink in the place. . . . Pesthole. Never had such duty in my life. Pleased to know you. Greyfuss is the name. . . . Not a drink in the place. Sit down, dammit. You're one of these dons we've been hearing about. What's wrong, eh? Dammit, if there's anything you want, speak up. We're here to keep order and we don't want any fighting. Hell of a post. Worst I've had since I was Old Rough and Ready's errand boy. No, sir, I don't hold a damn thing against you greasers in spite of the war. Lots of respect. But we've got to have order. Now what is it you want?"

49

Don Michael took the captain's offered cigarro and accepted the captain's light.

"*Señor el capitán,*" said the Irishman, "it is with great pleasure that I find so understanding a military officer here in Diablitos. I did not think such a fine gentleman would be utterly wasted upon such a dull position."

"My sentiments exactly," said Greyfuss with feeling.

"But," said *don* Michael with a languid wave of his hand toward the south, "it may not be quite as dull as you suspect."

"Why, dammit, it couldn't be worse. Drunks, flies, the rottenest scum of the frontier coming south and acting like they own the place. Land office mix-ups. It's *dull* enough!"

"Just now," said *don* Michael. "Later, say next Monday, it might prove a very exciting post indeed."

"Ah. You know of something coming off. Your *peónes* have told you of . . . what?"

"*Capitán,* your intelligence is quicker than one can parry. You have me there."

"And this trouble . . . ?"

"*Capitán,*" said *don* Michael, "it is not merely trouble. It is a war which is abrew."

"What?"

"Yes," said *don* Michael, slowly flicking the ashes from the cigarro and then taking a dreamy puff. "Yes, a war. On *la hacienda de* Obañon."

"Sure. I know. It's the hundred-thousand-acre Spanish land grant just south of here. A man named Lusby and another named Pearson have filed on it contingent upon railroad right of way."

"Obañon himself," said *don* Michael, "does not approve of those land claims of Lusby and Pearson. Obañon is going to fight."

Captain Greyfuss scrubbed his bearded jaw in agitation. "Dammit, that can't be allowed."

"Certainly not," said *don* Michael.

"But see here," said Greyfuss, "Obañon can't fight that way. An old Spanish grant is worthless. The border has moved and no Spanish grant, so far as I know, is going to be left the way it is."

"No *Spanish grant,* indeed," said *don* Michael. "Obañon knows that. But there is to be a war just the same. Monday."

"You know the actual time? Why, dammit, this is bad!"

"Obañon has imported munitions. Rifles and pistols to arm his *vaqueros.* But they cannot be found. Not now. If you were to go down to the rancho before this Monday, you would find only Lusby and Pearson and the others. But if you arrive Monday at nine o'clock in the evening, you can capture Obañon and his men."

"Why not before?"

"Because, *señor el capitán,* Obañon would then flee into the hills to be lost to you forever. He would snipe upon these men who have moved into the rancho. He would harass your towns and kill your people. This Obañon would be a bad man in such a position, *capitán.* You must come at nine o'clock next Monday night, arriving exactly at that moment. Then you can capture your Obañon with ease as he strives to attack the rancho. You can catch him between your lines and those of Lusby and Pearson and the country will remain peaceful. You will not forget this, *el capitán?*"

"Dammit, no! Thanks for the tip-off . . . Yes, yes. Thanks a great deal. Saves me no end of trouble. Much obliged."

Don Michael stood up and shook the captain's hand.

"And now," said *don* Michael, "I must go. I am delighted to know that such an intelligent officer was so fortunately on the ground."

Don Michael walked out to where Byles held his horse. He mounted, raised his hat, applied his spurs and dashed on up the street, leaving Captain Greyfuss to abruptly remember that he had not asked that charming fellow's name.

On the outskirts of Diablitos, *don* Michael slowed to a walk. A small 'dobe hut was just ahead and from it stepped a young Mexican with a glad grin. It was Antonio.

"*Don* Michael! You are still safe!"

"*Ai,* Antonio. Has anything come?"

"No, *don* Michael. Nothing."

"That is very bad, Antonio, my little one. You have watched for the post?"

"Yes. I have slept hardly at all, I have scarcely eaten!"

"Good. Watch well. As soon as the package comes, kill half a dozen horses if you must to get it to me. Upon it rests the fate of your people and *la hacienda de* Obañon."

"My life answers for it, *don* Michael."

"*Adios,* Antonio."

"*Adios, don* Michael."

CHAPTER EIGHT

CHARLIE PEARSON walked beside Julius Lusby in the hot light of Monday afternoon.

Lusby was sweating but his taste for dress would not allow him to undo his collar or unbutton his checkered vest. His little green hat sat precisely on his round head.

"But I tell you, Charlie, I don't want no killings!"

"To hell with what you want. We're being cold-decked, and that's a fact! Today we were to start a drive north with cattle. A crew like this ought to have gotten all the range cleared by this time, but they haven't. And today's the deadline for these damned disappearing artists to get the hell off our range. They had until today and unless every last one of them is gone, we're making a clean sweep."

"But Charlie, ain't it going to be hard to explain this to the government? Ain't it?"

"To hell with the government. We've spotted our claims and these greasers are still all over our land. I've seen them. Running like hell away from us whenever we've popped up and then vanishing like a sixth card in a poker hand. I'm through monkeying around. They're keeping cattle away from us and if we're going to pay all these gents that have filed in their names for us, we've got to have cash! And if we've got to have cash, we've got to drive cattle!"

"You mean it's a fight, huh?"

"What else can it be? But no," added Charlie as an afterthought—a thin grin on his thinner lips—"it won't be no fight."

"What do you mean, 'No fight'?"

Charlie spotted a thick, slovenly bruiser leaning against a corral gate. "Mudeye! Go tell the boys to start stirrin' around. We may have to get busy before sunset."

Mudeye lounged off toward the rows of 'dobe huts and Charlie turned back to Lusby.

"Of course there won't be no fight. It's goin' to be like runnin' sheep. Lefty Bill and Tex will be comin' back here in about an hour to tell us them greasers is all gone."

"Sure they will, Charlie. Didn't that *don* Michael ask nice to show 'em where to find all these Mexicans? That *don* Michael will tell 'em to get going and they'll go. You're gettin' all worked up over this, Charlie. We got about six thousand beeves, ain't it? We got enough to start that drive. And when the Mexicans all clear out, we'll get the rest and move in some more settlers and we'll be kings!"

"Yeah," said Charlie with a pleasurable grin. "That's right, ain't it, Julius? We got a spread as big as an eastern state. Yeah, I guess maybe I been workin' too hard shuffling for this deal. But when things get settled down, I'm goin' to relax. I'm goin' . . ."

"Who's that coming?" said Lusby, squinting up his eyes and staring through the blinding sunlight and heat waves of the plain.

They stood still, watching. Two of their riders were rocketing toward them, careening around the curves of the trail and raising a mountainous cloud of yellow dust.

"It's Tex and Lefty Bill!" said Charlie nervously. "Something's happened."

The horsemen drew sudden rein and their lathered mounts plunged. Tex, a stringy, leather-faced gunfighter jerked his thumb at Lefty Bill. The latter was holding on to his horn and had a green look around his mouth. Blood was staining his yellow shirt just under the shoulder.

"Lefty Bill's nicked!" said Tex unnecessarily.

"What happened?" demanded Charlie. "Where's that damned spiggoty you took along?"

Tex dismounted, easing his partner out of the saddle. "He left us at that ford south of here."

"Whatcha mean, left you?" said Lusby.

Tex had Lefty Bill on the ground. Other riders were coming up and crowding in. Two of them began to help Lefty Bill toward the ranch house.

"We got to th' ford all right and I asked th' greaser which way now and he said he thought we'd come far enough. He was real polite about it and Lefty Bill says, 'Hell, we ain't seen no greasers yet.' And this spiggoty smiles real nice and he says, 'You won't want to see none, boys. Be good and go back to the rancho.'

"And so I says, 'Where the hell do you think you're goin'?' And he says, 'If you don't mind, boys, I think I'll ride a ways further.' And he tips his hat to us and starts to send his horse into the water.

"Lefty Bill, he knows we ain't supposed to do nothin' like

this, so he yells, 'Hey, you. Come back here. We got to shoo these greasers the hell out of here and you ain't goin' no place without us.'

"Well, this spiggoty just grins and keeps goin'. So Lefty Bill grabs for his bowser like the forked lightnin' he is and WHAM! That *don* Michael gent must have eyes in the back of his noodle. Before Lefty Bill could drop his hammer, the spiggoty had turned around, drawed and let drive. The kick of the slug kicked Lefty Bill clean out of leather and he hits his backside on the ground and his horse bolts into mine so I can't sling lead.

"Then, when I gets ready for business I sees the muzzle of this spiggoty's six-gun on me so I knowed it wasn't no use. He says, 'I apologize, gentlemen. Pick up your friend, my thin bucko, and raise dust for the rancho.' Then he tips his hat again and turns around and crosses the ford and I picks up Lefty Bill and we burn trail for here, pronto."

Charlie was angry and his nostrils flared and quivered. "What's the idea lettin' him get away?"

"Hell," said Tex. "How'd I know we was supposed to guard him? He was so damned polite I thought he was a pal of yours, Mr. Pearson. How was I to know?"

"Is that all he said?" demanded Charlie.

"Well . . . no," hesitated Tex.

"Go on."

Tex took a deep breath. "He said, 'Tell Charlie a man can stand smellin' a polecat just so long and then he has to leave.'"

"He said that?" shouted Charlie.

"Well . . . just about that. But I couldn't remember exactly how he put it, it was so polite. But that's what he meant."

Mr. Lusby put his hand restrainingly on Charlie's arm. "Now, Charlie, we don't want . . ."

Charlie shook him off and faced the men. "Saddle your horses and get your guns. We're goin' to shoot every goddamn greaser we lay eyes on between now and sunset. Leave a dozen men here and don't bother the herd guards. How many in camp?"

"Ninety-one men," said Mudeye.

"That's enough to kill every greaser in Mexico," said Charlie. "By God, wait until I get my hands on that *don* Michael!"

CHAPTER NINE

THE sun at its zenith cast no shadows for rest in the *barrio del Bonifício,* built against the side of a craggy red mountain near the center of the vast valley of Santa Rosa.

Vaqueros in their gaudy boleros and sashes packed the small town, crowding every available foot of ground on the street and between the flat-roofed 'dobe houses. A long line of them, leading their mounts by the bridle, were filing slowly past four ox-carts which showed the signs of long travel.

Broken rifle cases were scattered about and others still intact were being pried open and dragged out. As each *vaquero* passed him, aged and wizened Enrico handed over a new rifle. Down the same line others were ladling out powder and bullets from kegs.

The *vaqueros* seized upon the weapons eagerly, their clean, lean faces expressing the joy and the relief they felt and their black eyes glowing.

Don Michael Patrick Obañon sat upon a big white stallion and watched the procedure. His mount restlessly stamped and shook his head and snorted and the silver conchas flashed and the curb bits jingled. But for all that activity, *don* Michael had a leg crooked around his solid silver horn and a cigarette held expressively in his right hand.

From time to time, *don* Michael would say, "Now you're

a fighter, Cristoforo," or "The *señoritas* will go mad, Pedro, absolutely mad!" And Cristoforo or Pedro or Tomaso would wave his new gun and shout, "*¡Viva don* Michael!" or "*¡Abajo los renegados!*" and go on to get his bullets and powder and caps.

As the line neared its end and as the broken cases almost obscured Enrico, a wild-eyed young Hispano-Apache with black hair streaming and sombrero on only by grace of his chin thong stormed into the *barrio*.

"*¡Los renegados!*" he shouted as he came. "*¡Vengan los renegados!*"

He jerked to a stop before *don* Michael. "They are here! I have seen them! They come as the sky-blackening geese from the rancho!"

"Calm," said *don* Michael, putting his foot back into his stirrup and throwing the cigarette away. "Not as geese blackening the sky, my excited one. As coyotes sniffing the earth with their yellow bellies in the dust. They saw you?"

"No," said the boy indignantly. "Am I wholly a white man?"

Don Michael laughed musically and the *vaqueros,* after an undecided moment, joined in. The tension was broken.

"And now," said *don* Michael, "all our fine women and *niños* are far to the south and in no danger and all we must do is to outwit these mighty warriors. Before nightfall, *amigos míos,* they shall be shivering in their jackboots, eh?"

"*¡Ai!*" roared two hundred throats. "*¡Viva don* Michael!"

Vaqueros hurled themselves to horse and eagerly turned in the direction from which the boy had come.

Don Michael was smiling, amused. "It would be very pretty to charge them, my brave gentlemen. But that would not be very good sense. Come, we trot very slowly around the mountain and to the east, slowly so as not to raise the dust."

Enrico lowered his brows in wonder. "Why, *don* Michael?"

"Enrico, my old and ancient friend," said *don* Michael, "I think there is enough Apache in you, or at least enough devil, to know 'why.' Don't tell me, Enrico, that you do not trust me."

"*¡Viva don* Michael!" bellowed from two hundred throats.

"Lead, *don* Michael," smiled Enrico. "I follow though you go to the very gates of the Forbidden Land."

Don Michael's stallion snorted as the rein tightened and the spurs touched. At a trot, the cavalcade began to move away from the still-unseen *renegados*.

CHAPTER TEN

A T the rancho, Lusby squatted in the desk chair and clutched a pen. His face was filled with a serene joy which was touching to behold. He was making figures on a sheet which bore the beautiful engraved crest of the Obañons.

"Eight thousand beeves," he muttered, scribbling, "at maybe thirty dollars . . . is two hundred . . . sure. Two hundred and forty thousand dollars . . ." He grinned expansively and seemed to grow in size as he fondly repeated the sum. "Two hundred and forty thousand dollars! And to think that twenty years ago I was peddling!"

His face clouded and he unhooked his thumbs from his checkered vest. "Two hundred and forty thousand dollars. Let's see. That two into it, one hundred and twenty thousand dollars makes. And then there's the boys, feed, trail drivers . . ."

He looked a little worried and the pen scratched faster as the pressure was applied.

Tex was sitting across the room, listening half-heartedly. Lefty Bill, on the couch, was showing signs of improvement, perhaps attributable to the almost-empty Madeira bottle beside him, a bottle which also bore the Obañon crest of arms.

"At forty dollars a month . . ." muttered Lusby.

Tex looked vacantly at the bottle. "I wisht they'd taken me along. I would have showed them damned greasers a thing or two."

Lefty Bill moved a little and his pudgy face twitched. "Yeah. I notice how you plugged that spiggoty after he got me."

"Damn it, he was so all-fired polite I didn't half know what was happenin' until it was done," said Tex. "And how could I 'a' drawed when he had me covered?"

"You coulda drawed when I did," growled Lefty Bill.

"Two hundred and . . ." muttered Lusby.

"Sure I coulda," said Tex. "But with him faced one way and ridin' one minute and then faced t'other and shootin' back the next split second and with yore hoss atryin' to use me for a ladder, what could I 'a' done? Huh? Answer me that? What could I 'a' done?"

"I think you was scared out of your pants," stated Lefty Bill.

"Scared? Me scared? Of a guy like that? Why, I never seed no dandy yet that had a bit of spunk in him. Him with that silver hat and them silver-plated pants of his'n! Huh, I bet he uses enough perfume. . . ."

"I never smelled none on him."

"Well, he might use it anyhow. Them silk shirts he wears with the blousey sleeves and that silver-plated gun. Huh! Scared of a done-up dude like that? Me?"

"Yeah, you."

"If you wasn't flat on yore back I'd show you a thing or two, Mr. Lefty Bill Stevens. Any guy that'd wear a sombrero like he does can't fight. Say, I wonder how much one of them things costs. I bet a couple hundred bucks anyway. You s'pose a man could get one in Kansas City, huh?"

"You thinkin' of buyin' one?" said Lefty Bill.

". . . and a half . . ." muttered Lusby.

"Me? Wear a thing like that? I should *say* not! And them boots of his'n. I bet they don't weigh an ounce apiece. Absolutely no good atall . . . Bet they was tailor made. Wonder if you could buy a pair of *them* in Kansas City?"

"I told you. The guy had you scared green!"

"He did not! Why, if he was to come in here this minute I'd whip out my bowser and . . ."

BOW!

All three men in the room gave a start. The shot had been fired from somewhere near the corrals. It took chips out of the far wall.

BOW! BAM! BAM! BOW, BOW, BOW! SCREEEEEE!

"What the hell!" shouted Tex, leaping up, gun in hand. Through the window he could see some of his friends sprinting for the corral and turning to fire back at something lost to view beyond the 'dobe huts.

Puffs of dirt were leaping up about these gentlemen's boots but the firing did not seem to be effective as none of them dropped despite the rolling thunder of rifle shots.

Lusby had been at his desk a moment before. He was gone.

Tex looked at the empty chair, bewildered. Lefty Bill was trying to struggle up from the couch and get at a rifle which dangled above him on pegs.

PAM! BOW, BAM! SCREEEeeeeeeee! BLOOEY! POW, BAM!

65

"Lusby!" shouted Tex. "Where the hell . . . ?"

He caught sight of a heel sticking out from under a big table and seized it to haul Lusby out.

"I give up!" yowled Lusby, shivering. He turned over on the floor and saw it was Tex.

CRACK! BAM, POW!

"What's happenin'?" begged Lusby.

Tex went to the window. Most of the men who had been running were now mounted. Two of them were still struggling with unruly horses.

"Wait!" wailed Tex, bolting for the door. "Hey! Wait for me!"

He jerked the latch to him and the door banged back against the wall.

Tex froze in his tracks. His gun drooped in his hand and then dropped to the floor. He backed up very slowly, the hair on the back of his neck sticking out straight.

Don Michael stepped inside and looked quietly around the room. He pinwheeled his bright revolver and grinned, his blue eyes very merry.

"Pardon, *señores*. I obstruct your passage. Do you not wish to leave with your friends?"

Lusby sat in the middle of the floor, jaw hanging open. Tex backed against the table for support. Lefty Bill gave up trying to get at the gun and just glared.

"But forgive me," said *don* Michael. "I do not blame you for not wanting to leave. It is so very hot."

"I thought you was goin' to plug him next time," jeered Lefty Bill.

Tex made no sign that he had heard except to bring his hands conspicuously free from his sides.

A drumming sound was in the air and the room trembled.

Don Michael went over to the desk where sat a decanter of brandy. He caught sight of the page of figures.

"Two hundred and forty thousand dollars," he said musingly. He poured a small drink. "I really had no idea, *señor* Lusby."

"What . . . what you going to do?" said Lusby.

Don Michael shrugged. "It is now four o'clock. Soon your friends will tire of searching for the 'cowardly greaser.' They will come home. . . ."

Lusby scrambled up and tried to bolt for the door now that the gun was not upon him. *Don* Michael snaked out a boot and Lusby went down again.

"They will come home," said *don* Michael, "and then we shall have a party. If you, me thin bucko, wish to stay, by all means stay. If you wish to go, tell *señor* Pearson that I have changed my mind."

"Changed your mind?" croaked Tex.

"Yes," said *don* Michael. "He is not a *Mephitis mephitica,* or common skunk, but a *Zeminis constrictor.*"

"A . . . a . . . huh?"

"A variety of snake which eats itself," said *don* Michael.

"Y . . . y'mean I can go?" shivered Tex. "Y'won't shoot me down if I try to run for it? Y'men won't kill me?"

Don Michael stepped to the door. "*¡Oye!* Let this one also go!"

Tex waited not for another invitation. He sprinted across

the porch and through the flower beds, leaped the wall at the far end and streaked for the corrals. A few seconds later he was outward bound, still trying to mount, the terrifying vision of at least two hundred brightly clothed and armed *vaqueros* jeering him on his way.

Don Michael came back into the room and looked at Lefty Bill. "My apologies, *señor*. I did not mean to hit you quite so hard. An inch above that spot there is a layer of soft muscle. I regret that my hasty action, perhaps prompted in some measure by your own commendable swiftness of the draw, made it necessary for such a hasty bullet on my part."

"Save it," growled Lefty Bill. "If y'gonna kill me now, quit playin' with me and get it over with."

"My dear fellow," said *don* Michael. "You amaze me."

"If you wouldn't use such big words," said Lefty Bill, "maybe I'd know what you was talkin' about."

Enrico came to the door and took off his hat before he entered.

Don Michael looked up. "Enrico. Get some water hot and bring me my medicine case. This gentleman needs a little patching."

"*Sí, don* Michael." But he lingered. "*Don* Michael . . ."
"Yes?"

"*Don* Michael, it is with great sorrow that I witnessed the bad shooting of our men. They know little about guns, *don* Michael. I was ashamed. They make the noise but not the execution. Not one *renegado* did they hit just now. Not one," he added with a sob in his voice.

"The hot water," said *don* Michael.

"*Sí*. I go."

Lusby recovered his voice. "C . . . c . . . can I go, too?"

"I regret," said *don* Michael, "that you cannot. However, make yourself at home."

"Y . . . y . . . you mean you're goin' to lie here and ambush all my men? You'll kill them all off?"

"Having sent ten or eleven potential messengers to warn them and after that exhibition of bad shooting? No, *señor* Lusby, unless a very remarkable thing happens, all the casualties will be on my side."

Enrico came back. "*Don* Michael. Jorge gets the hot water."

"Good. Enrico, go out and begin to post the men. Group them about the house in positions where they cannot be easily hit. I shall inspect them in a little while."

"*Sí, don* Michael. I hear and I go."

"Say," said Lusby in a doubtful tone. "Who are you anyhow?"

Don Michael smiled a little but it was a proud smile.

"*Señor*, I am Michael Patrick Obañon, an Irish gentleman."

CHAPTER ELEVEN

EVENING dragged into night and still nothing happened. *Don* Michael paced about the garden walls, where the *vaqueros* had ambitiously punched out loopholes, greeted by enthusiasm everywhere. But it was a nervous, strained enthusiasm. The men had seen the smallness of effect their shots had had and a great deal of their confidence in their marksmanship had evaporated. Never in their lives had they ever had any use for firearms. They could protect themselves ably in fights with the knives which they could throw accurately enough to split toothpicks at ten paces. They could use a riata with the same precision other men could use bullets. A handful had had experience in the war, but they were only half a dozen among two hundred.

Padre Ramon stopped *don* Michael beside the gate. "My son, this is murder. What chance have these men against trained killers? I too saw the effect of their shots, or I should say lack of effect. Is there nothing we can do to prevent this?"

Don Michael glanced toward the east where the moon was rising in an orange sheet of fire. "It is already nine, *padre*. I had hoped . . . But no. Of course these things can never go right. At least it is better than running away."

He moved on and stopped beside Enrico, who had muffled himself against the growing cold with his serape.

"There is no sign of Antonio?" said *don* Michael.

"The two men you sent have not come back," replied the aged major-domo.

"The Fates," said *don* Michael, "are not being very kind."

"What is delaying the *renegados*?" said Enrico, peering out into the darkness. "They have had time to get back and the outposts report nothing." He was uneasy. "*Don* Michael, do you not have a feeling of disaster?"

"Disaster?" said *don* Michael. "With two hundred brave *vaqueros* armed to the teeth? You jest, Enrico."

The moon's glow was stronger, painting the valley with a weird, penetrating light, making the square 'dobe huts throw long ebon shadows against the blue-white earth.

Don Michael made the rounds again, restlessly stopping every few feet to peer over the wall into the open. He passed his hand across his eyes and found that his palm was sweaty. Until that moment he had not realized how nervous he was.

"They do not come," complained Tomaso. "*Don* Michael, is there something wrong?"

"Wrong?" said *don* Michael. "Of course not, my witless ape. They know we are here and they know how fearless we are. They have the good sense not to charge us."

"You think so?" said Tomaso, glowing.

Don Michael walked on.

They had turned most of their horses out into the open. The big white stallion lingered near the corrals, thinking of oats. He gave a sudden snort and raised his head, ears standing alert and staring across the moonlit plain.

Don Michael watched him.

The stallion moved a few paces and then stopped to stare at something again. Abruptly he plunged away at a run to vanish beyond the stables.

Don Michael eased a long French rifle over the wall. He squeezed the trigger as delicately as though he handled glass. Flame stabbed from the muzzle and then white smoke rolled outward with the crashing report.

Through it, *don* Michael dimly saw a man stand straight upright beside the church. He posed there for an instant, one arm outflung as though to start a speech. As unbendable as wood, he thudded to the earth.

At half a dozen different places, red eyes blinked open. The volley came as thunder an instant later, and *don* Michael brushed sleeve to cheek where masonry had stung him.

Four or five *vaqueros* convulsively jerked their triggers in ragged succession. All was still for the space of a breath. The storm broke.

The squat, square 'dobes glowed from the splashing scarlet of powder flame. The outside wall of the garden was painted about its whole perimeter with lightning.

After that first ear-crushing din, the firing grew spasmodic as men loaded and fired at will. The night was lanced apart by ricochets which shrilled like breaking harpstrings.

"*¡Ai, Dios mío!*" whimpered Tomaso.

"Jesus!" screamed someone by the corral.

Half-blind by flaring powder and choked by caustic fumes, *don* Michael went swiftly along the line. "Steady. Aim before you fire. Load with care. There is no hurry. They dare not charge. *Ai,* Cristoforo, you are a man to

73

stand it without wincing. And how you can proudly limp before the *señoritas*! Steady. Load carefully. See, this is how it is done. . . . WHAM . . . See, he dropped. It is nothing . . . Enrico, get this man into the house. . . . Beautiful, Miguel, how neatly you drilled him. . . . Steady, Jorge. Take your time. Where is the ramrod? . . . Ah, of course. How could you remember to take it out and not fire it away? Very well, it's wrapped about some *renegado's* neck. . . . See, Jorge, you hold this in the left hand and . . . Ah, yes, it *would* be nicer to use the knife but we are too far. You will have your chance. . . . Enrico, get this man back to the house. . . . Of course they fire fast. But wait until they charge. They cannot load then. . . . Steady. Aim before you fire. Beautiful moon, isn't it, Ricardo. . . . All right, Enrico, I shall get down. . . . Steady. Aim before you . . . *That* was a fine one. Keep them off that roof. You fight like you knew how. . . . Steady. Aim before . . . Keep them off that roof! Don't let them shoot down into here! Give me that rifle. . . . There. You see how it is done? Drop them as they come over the top of that ladder. . . . Higher, Jose. We plow the fields, not our front yard. You want me to plant something there, eh? Good boy. That was better. . . ."

"Antonio," said Enrico, "can never get through to us even if he does come."

"He's not the only one that's late," replied *don* Michael. "It is nine-thirty at least. They'll get up nerve to charge soon and they've all got revolvers. Enrico, tell the men to lay their knives handy. This is going to be close."

"*Don* Michael, if they charge, we can never stop them once they're over that wall. Revolvers . . ."

"We can do no less than try, Enrico."

"*Sí, don* Michael."

"Enrico . . ."

An invisible sledge hammer crashed into *don* Michael. He staggered sideways, his lean face tightened with shock, his eyes hard shut.

"*Don Michael!*"

He slumped into Enrico's supporting arms.

CHAPTER TWELVE

CHARLIE PEARSON crouched at the rear of the blacksmith shop, hot rifle in his sure, long fingers. Beside him crouched the man known as Mudeye and, beyond him, Tex.

"I think I got him," said Charlie. "Let's see if he can get that one out of his deck."

"Looky," said Tex, "the fire's dyin' down."

Charlie's face was wolfish, painted by the blue light of the moon. "I reckon that calls the turn, gents. Pass the word. We're goin' in there and mop up."

"Y' think we can get across that open?" said Mudeye.

"Only two or three of them gents and that damned spiggoty been throwin' sevens and I done for *him*." Charlie faced them. "Pass the word."

Mudeye crawled off on his belly to contact the unevenly spaced line.

"Y' s'pose they killed Lusby?" said Tex.

"Good riddance if they did. I'm sick of him. This moppin' ought to be a lead-pipe cinch. We'll take them all on this side and get the others from behind."

"I can't see so good," said Tex. "Got sand in my eyes."

"You better get some sand in your guts, skinny."

"But ain't they got knives?"

77

"What's a knife against a Walker pistol, huh?" demanded Charlie.

Mudeye came wriggling back. "They're waitin' for you, Pearson."

Charlie stood up. "I ain't waitin' for nothin'! LET'S GO!"

Into the brilliant moonlight sprang the attackers, rifles cast aside, pistols in hand. A racketing shout bayed from eighty throats.

Charlie lunged forward into the open, his dense shadow sweeping across the hard-packed sand.

All eyes were upon the garden walls ahead. Otherwise that which happened would never have occurred.

CRACK! BAM! SCREEeeeeee! CRACK!

Not Spanish rifles and not from the walls ahead. Sharp, spiteful carbines made that sound. Carbines and Colt's Army.

To the right and out of the ground leaped a hundred men on dashing horses, vanguarded by their powder flame, gigantic and terrifying in the moonlight. Guidons whipping, hoofs rolling, sabers flashing in the moonlight.

And over the din shrilled the staccato, thrilling notes of a cavalry bugle sounding the CHARGE!

Blue coats and bright buttons. Black hats with brims plastered back by speed. A rolling, deafening battle cry sounding CHARGE!

Out of the plains they came, riding hard and recklessly, leaning half out of their saddles and straining ahead with the wind whooshing as it was knifed by their saber blades. Mounts' manes streaming like the guidons, hard hoofs rolling like kettle drums. And nearer and nearer came the hysterical brassy notes of that bugle sounding CHARGE!

Not ten feet on their way, the *renegados* stopped still, staring in amazement and terror, so many moonlight-outlined statues frozen still in the attitudes of running.

And then Charlie Pearson knew that he and his men were the targets of that cavalry onslaught. He lifted his voice in the thunderous din.

"STOP! STOP FOR GOD'S SAKE! WE'RE AMERICANS!"

Renegados went down, too stiffened with amazement to fire a return shot, too frozen for the moment to even run.

On swept the tide of cavalry, closer to them, almost into the buildings. . . .

The *renegados* shrieked a concerted wail of despair, whirled and pounded their heavy boots against the sand.

Suddenly the first rank of cavalry pulled sharply up. The speed was out of their eyes and the moonlight was bright. Ahead they could see red shirts and beards and men with Walker pistols.

"CAPTAIN!" screamed a lieutenant. "RECALL! THEY'RE WHITE MEN!"

In the instant the bugle changed its tune. Troopers piled up into the first ranks which were plowing to a stop. Horses, mad with speed, fought their bits. Sabers were cast away so as to do less harm in the jumble. Colts were swiftly holstered and carbines booted.

Greyfuss, a powerful figure on a lunging black horse, held up his hand! "LEFT FLANK WHEEL!"

Order came out of chaos. The troopers plunged into the protection of the buildings.

Charlie bounced out of cover, voice tight and hoarse with rage. "Are you blind? Can't you hear? My God, you've ruined everything!"

"Pearson," said Greyfuss in astonishment. "But I was told . . . I thought the greasers were attacking you! I was told *you* were in the *hacienda*! What . . . what's this all about?"

"By God, after what you've done, you've got to help me now. That damned spiggoty's got a couple hundred greasers in there, all of them armed. . . ."

A lieutenant was saluting for attention. "Sir, they've got a white flag up on the wall."

Greyfuss turned and looked. The flag was certainly there.

Charlie stared at it in hopeless disappointment. "Surrendered," he spat. "Just when we had them. . . . By God, that *don* Michael better not be alive. . . ."

CHAPTER THIRTEEN

D ON MICHAEL was sitting in his drawing room and the chair in which he sat was high-backed and emblazoned with the Obañon crest. His left arm was in a sling and his face, in contrast to the jet of his hair, was very white. But there was flash to his eyes and a quirk of a smile upon his lips as he watched Captain Greyfuss, two other officers, Charlie Pearson and Judge Klarner come thumping in.

Enrico stood at the side of *don* Michael's chair, his old eyes blazing like an eagle's and his face very stern.

Greyfuss switched dust around as he angrily yanked off his cavalry gloves. He looked searchingly through the candlelit room, as though unwilling to immediately fix his mind on *don* Michael.

"You," said Greyfuss. "What's the meaning of all this?"

Don Michael nodded politely. "May I introduce myself, Captain. I am Michael Patrick Obañon."

"Obañon?" snapped Charlie. "Obañon? Why, you . . ."

Greyfuss thrust his hand out to restrain Pearson. Greyfuss spoke in his court-martial voice.

"Obañon, this is a very grave thing you have done. A *very* grave thing. You are guilty of bearing arms against a friendly people. You are guilty of arming a cutthroat crew for lawless purposes. And, furthermore, you are guilty of murder. It is my solemn duty to take you into custody for trial. . . ."

Don Michael indicated a table which was set with cigars and wine glasses. "Relax, Captain. You must be dry after a hard ride. Sit down and get your breath back and then we can go on with this."

Greyfuss glared horribly.

Judge Klarner noisily cleared his throat. "I knew you would come to this, Michael. I told you. . . ."

"I see they let you loose, *señor el juez,*" smiled *don* Michael.

Klarner turned red. "Yes. Of course they let me loose. I am naturally obliged to you for assuming full responsibility for the murder of Gus Mueller. Naturally, very indebted." He drew down his bushy white brows. "Indeed, I am indebted. But had you taken my advice instead of following this lawless and scatterbrained course, you would now be free, in possession of some of your land instead of en route to the gallows, instead of bearing the stigma of a bandit."

"Won't *you* have some wine, *señor el juez?*"

Klarner stood where he was, unmoving, reproof in his every feature.

The captain had opened his mouth to speak again when Lusby burst out of the bedroom. His hair was standing straight up and his face was polished with sweat.

"Charlie!" cried Lusby. "You got the gov'munt! That's *him.* That's him there! That's Obañon! Thank God you got here before the fiend murdered . . ."

"Shut up," said Charlie. "What about this, Captain? Do I

get a hand in taking him in? I got enough evidence against this gent to swing him higher'n a kite."

"Of course," said *don* Michael. "Captain, by all means, give *señor* Pearson the satisfaction of helping to take me to Diablitos. I fear I have been the cause of great aggravation to him."

"I won't need any help," vowed Greyfuss.

"I apologize, *el capitán*," smiled *don* Michael, "for the misinformation which so regrettably led you to charge and kill some of our countrymen and I quite sympathize with your hostility."

Greyfuss did not seem to appreciate the polite tone. He glared fiercely. "You planned that trap. You knew these bandits of yours, armed to the teeth, minds inflamed with murder, would take this rancho and cause me to make that blunder."

"Yes," said *don* Michael, reaching for a cigarro. "I seem to remember that I did." Enrico held the match for him.

"This country," growled Greyfuss, "can get along without your despicable kind."

"Well, what the hell are we waiting for?" snapped Charlie. "The cards are dealt and this spiggoty held the low hand. Let's go."

"A moment," said *don* Michael mildly as they started to move toward him. "Before we leave the rancho, there is one charge of which I am not guilty. Shall we clear it up, gentlemen?"

"You got plenty of charges!" said Lusby. "You got enough charges to fill a ledger! You played us for a bunch of fools!"

He was most truculent, there between two armed lieutenants of cavalry. "Whatever you got comin', you got comin' and no more monkey business!"

Don Michael's smile was very odd. "This one charge cannot wait, gentlemen, as the evidence is here. Enrico, please bring me that sandalwood box from the compartment of my desk."

"Hell," said Charlie, "are you goin' to stand here all night? He ain't got nothin' to show you. He's stalling for time. All he's holdin' is a pair of deuces. Let's go!"

Enrico came back with the sandalwood box and gave it to *don* Michael. For a moment the captain's curiosity held the upper hand.

Don Michael handed the box to Greyfuss. "Open it, *el capitán*."

Greyfuss impatiently lifted the lid and looked in. "What's this all about? There's nothing but a bullet in here."

"Yes," said *don* Michael, "nothing but a bullet."

"Come on," said Charlie irritably. "What the hell are we waitin' for?"

"That bullet originally," said *don* Michael, "came out of a Derringer, caliber forty-one."

"Obviously," said Greyfuss. "But I fail to see . . ."

"A little later," continued *don* Michael, "it came out of the corpse of Gus Mueller—and if you exhume the body I think you will be able to fit the bullet into a hole where it was embedded in bone. I regret the necessity of that autopsy—"

"What's this all about?" growled Greyfuss. "You've confessed to the man's murder already. I see no reason . . ."

"Ah," cautioned *don* Michael. "I did nothing of the sort.

I merely assumed the responsibility for it, indicating that I would deliver up, not myself, but the murderer."

"Hell, he's stretchin' them deuces too damned far," snapped Charlie. "Let's go!"

"A Derringer forty-one, you say?" said Greyfuss. "That was the only bullet in Mueller?"

"Yes," smiled *don* Michael. "And the only Derringer in camp at the time of his death belonged to *señor* Pearson, who took the happy opportunity to kill a man he thought menaced his control of the rancho. Am I correct, Mr. Pearson?"

Charlie grinned suddenly. "That's the smoothest bluff I ever saw pulled. I got to hand it to you, Spiggoty. When you got the cards you can sure play 'em. It'll be a loss to the gamblin' profession when they march you up the thirteen steps for banditry and murder and the slaughter of citizens as well as the illegal importation of arms and ammunition. I sure hate to see such a good poker player swing. Come on, Captain."

Greyfuss tossed the box and bullet to the table, upsetting a wine glass. "I did not see the bullet come out of the body and it would be easy for you to recover such a slug and present it. Besides, there are far graver charges than murder facing you, Obañon. Gentlemen, lead the fellow to a horse."

Don Michael took a long drag on the cigarro and then tamped it carefully out. The two lieutenants moved in on either side of him to pull him out of the chair. Charlie Pearson was grinning widely but in Lusby's eyes there was a question as he gazed upon his partner.

"I'm sorry," said Klarner. "If there's anything I can do for you while you're waiting trial, let me know."

"Generous of you," said *don* Michael politely.

Greyfuss was drawing on his gloves. "Come on. We've waited long enough."

Don Michael was helped to his feet. He stood there, paler than ever, a faint smile on his lips, his eyes fixed on a point through and beyond them—the door.

Antonio was standing there, young face set, black eyes frightened. In his hand he held a big yellow envelope.

"Come in, Antonio," said *don* Michael.

The crowd turned and stared impatiently. The boy stared through them at *don* Michael. "You are shot!"

"Ai," said *don* Michael. "And almost hanged. The envelope, Antonio."

Don Michael sat down again and stretched out his legs. He lighted another cigarro and then began to break the seals of the envelope.

"Another bluff!" snapped Charlie, disgusted.

"Obañon," threatened Greyfuss, "I can be pushed too far. It will be dawn before we get back to Diablitos now. Dammit, man, get up and let's get out of here!"

Don Michael blew out smoke and ruffled the contents of the packet. Then he extended the entire sheaf to Greyfuss.

"Your voice," said *don* Michael, "is most excellent, *el capitán*. Please read some of these aloud."

Suspiciously Greyfuss fastened on to the papers. He glared at the first sheet and then incredulity began to seep into his stare. His jaw gradually slacked and abruptly snapped shut. He looked at *don* Michael and then back at the papers.

"Read, *el capitán*," said *don* Michael, wickedly.

Greyfuss appeared most uncomfortable, but he cleared his throat and read,

My dear Mr. Obañon:

I trust the Pony Express and special messengers will get these documents to you in time. We are only too glad to place our firm at the disposal of the son of Timothy Obañon. We enclose a voucher to acknowledge the receipt of monies as hereafter explained, part of which we have devoted to this work which, because of its speed, was expensive. May we have the pleasure of further serving you in the future.

Blankenship and Blankenship,
Attorneys at Law,
Washington, DC

"Blankenship and Blankenship?" gaped Klarner. "Why . . . why, my God, they're the biggest outfit in the capital. It costs thousands just to talk to them. How . . . ?"

"I fail to see how this will change matters," said Greyfuss, trying to retain his severity.

"Read on, *el capitán*," said *don* Michael, very gravely.

Greyfuss turned a page. His eyes popped wide and he then blinked them rapidly. "Why . . . why, dammit, this is a birth certificate. . . . You aren't a greaser! You're an Irishman! You're a citizen of the United States."

"A detail," said *don* Michael. "Continue, *el capitán*. I have never heard such elocution in my life. What a splendid voice timbre! Read on."

Greyfuss began to feel uneasy but he bravely turned another page and read,

> As initial payment for deeding a strip two miles wide and twenty and a half miles long across the plains to the north of and on the property of *la hacienda de* Obañon, payment is hereby acknowledged from the Sante Fe Railway Company, the sum of thirty-two thousand dollars.
>
> Blankenship and Blankenship

With an explosive bark, Greyfuss cried, "You can't sell this land! It has been filed upon by Pearson and Lusby. You're mad! No Spanish land grant has so far been upheld! You . . ."

Don Michael smiled sweetly. "Go on, *el capitán*, your voice is the most beautiful music I have heard in weeks. Next page, please."

Greyfuss sputtered and turned the sheet, angered by his seeming inability to make a dent in *don* Michael. "'Synopsis of notes from . . .' What's this?" He looked aghast at *don* Michael. "'Synopsis of notes and telegrams . . .'" He gulped audibly. "'From the *Presidente de Mejico* to the President of the United States concerning the person and property of one Michael Patrick Obañon.'" Greyfuss turned scarlet, swallowed again and charged ahead with great effort.

> The Valley of Santa Rosa, as herein documented, was deeded to one Timothy Obañon in consideration of payment and services to the Republic of *Mejico* and is therefore an outright, deeded purchase with clear title to the extent of one hundred thousand acres. . . .

He could not go on.

"I said," smiled *don* Michael, "that no *Spanish grant* was reliable. I need not point out the validity of my title to *la hacienda de* Obañon. It is not a Spanish grant."

Greyfuss was flopping his gloves weakly and his face was very, very red. Lusby and Pearson were transfixed.

"Read on," said *don* Michael, soothingly.

Greyfuss turned another sheet. "'All land titles,'" he choked, "'except that of Michael Patrick Obañon, are therefore false . . .'"

"Read on," said *don* Michael, gently. "I did not expect the last paper."

Greyfuss looked at it. The hair literally stood up on his head. He made three attempts to read and failed in each. Finally he drew a gusty breath and said, "Why . . . why dammit . . . My God . . . this is a letter from . . . from the President of the United States . . . in . . . informing you of his past connection . . . connection with your father and . . . and appointing . . . appointing you LIEUTENANT GOVERNOR OF THE TERRITORY OF NEW MEXICO!"

The only thing in the room which moved was the lazily coiling smoke which rose ceilingward from *don* Michael's select cigarro.

Abruptly Pearson made a break for the door. But a foot brought him down and the troopers held him there.

Klarner dabbed weakly at his face with a polka-dot handkerchief, muttering over and over, ". . . and I came out . . . I came out to help a man . . . like that."

Greyfuss recovered himself. He clicked his heels as sharply as a pistol shot, his face a grave, military mask.

"Sir," said Greyfuss to *don* Michael, "I regret the trouble to which you and your brave *vaqueros* have been placed. If there is anything which you wish me to do, you have only to send for me. Myself and my troops are at your command."

He saluted briskly and executed a precise about-face, heading for the door. Out of the corner of his mouth he barked, "Get these two damned renegades and come on."

The lieutenants scooped up Charlie Pearson and Lusby and shoved them into the hands of waiting troopers.

"You low-lifer!" said Lusby harshly, glaring at Charlie. "I told you he was a gentleman!"

STORY PREVIEW

STORY PREVIEW

NOW that you've just ventured through one of the captivating tales in the Stories from the Golden Age collection by L. Ron Hubbard, turn the page and enjoy a preview of *Under the Diehard Brand*. Join Lee Thompson, who must step in to help his father regain control over gunslinging town troublemakers. But when he arrives, Lee finds that he may be forced to abandon the rule of law, leaving his father's reputation as sheriff hanging in the balance.

UNDER THE
DIEHARD BRAND

THE night rider was nervous. It was with considerable effort that he kept his voice easy and assured as he sang. Two thousand longhorns, bedded down on the strange range country of Montana, moved restively, still upset after the dangerous crossing of the Missouri that day.

Summer lightning flashed in bright brass sheets along the horizon, momentarily showing up the semicircle of rimrock which surrounded the bed ground. The mutter of thunder growled across the sky. Bunched-up clouds shot nervously across the face of the moon.

The weary young trail hand knew there would be trouble before morning.

> "Sit down little cyows
> And rest yo' tails,
> An' forgit all about them dusty trails.
> Now if you played faro
> Or had a rival to yo' gal
> Yo' worries would be . . ."

He stopped suddenly and looked questioningly at the ridge to the south. Sheet lightning silhouetted a rider up there.

The trail hand rode a short distance from his charges to wave the strange horseman off from the nervous herd. The rider was coming slowly down the slope, being very careful to ride easily and quietly.

The trail hand advanced. "Howdy, stranger. Step light. These bovines is nervous wrecks after our crossin' today." He studied the other but asked no questions. He saw that the horse was travel-worn and knew from the other's rig and clothes that he had come through from Texas—which is a long jump.

"Sure. But they been mighty sparin' of signposts and I don't savvy this country none. Where's Wolf River?"

The trail hand looked more closely and saw that the stranger was young, around eighteen, and from the looks of him hadn't eaten very regularly of late. "The wagon's over to your right, stranger. Better go over and git down. We're short-handed and might be able to help you along."

"Thanks, but I been comin' for such a hell of a while that I'm gettin' anxious to see the target. You know Wolf River?"

"Some."

"Know if I can find Diehard Thompson there?"

"Sure you can. Last I hear of him, he's sheriff."

"Gettin' along all right?" said the stranger.

"Gettin' along in age," replied the trail hand. "Was a time when strong men fainted at the mention of that name, but the old boy's agin' up pretty bad. One of these days, somebody is goin' to get nerve enough to find out if he's as bulletproof as he used to be. He's slippin'. There's plenty of citizens—"

"Wait a minute," said the stranger, "you're talkin' about my dad."

"Hell, no offense, I hope. I didn't know Diehard ever

stopped practicin' the draw long enough to have a kid." He stopped uncomfortably. "Cooky'll fix you up if you drop over. You'd be plumb welcome to drift north with us, Thompson."

The youngster shifted wearily in his saddle and the trail hand noted the absence of all weapons.

"Guess I'll be swingin' on if you'll wise me up."

"Sure. Keep the Pole Star on your left a little. Wolf River's about sixty miles and if you miss it you'll fall over the GN tracks."

"Much obliged. Be seein' you."

The kid started a wide circle around the herd, picking his way by the flare of lightning. He was very thoughtful and a frown wrinkled up his tired face.

He traveled until he reached the other side of the bed ground and then looked up to pick out the Pole Star. Clouds were scudding across it, yellow in the lightning, blue white in the moonlight, and the task was difficult.

He had just singled it out when, behind him, he heard the far-off crack of a shot, almost blotted out by the summer thunder. He turned in his saddle and looked back.

He could see the whole amphitheater from where he sat. The cattle had started up, looking about, beginning to walk nervously in small circles.

He knew one rider could not hold that herd now and he reined around, intending to go back and be of what help he could.

Another shot made a thin red line on the ridge across.

The kid saw the trail hand as lightning fanned across the horizon. The man was laying on his quirt, racing away from the evident ambush, toward the far-off chuck wagon, going for help. The puncher streaked up the slope toward the ridge not far from the kid. The roll of the mustang's hoofs came faintly above the growing rumble in the herd.

An instant later, half a dozen horsemen rose magically on the rim above the trail hand, as black and stiff as though they had been cut from cardboard.

A heavyset fellow on a chunky horse spurred down to meet the puncher. Orange flame spat. Lightning flared.

The puncher leaned backwards in his saddle, hands thrown up. He vanished and his horse plunged on.

An instant later the others on the ridge started down, firing into the air, shouting.

The herd was ready to go. With a roll which shook the earth, two thousand longhorns began to stampede.

The cracking shots were blotted out in the crash of horns against horns. The riders were swallowed up in the geysering black dust.

The kid dug spur toward the unseen chuck wagon, quirting his weary horse. But his message was not needed. The fire was kicked together and tired men were struggling up, grabbing saddles and rifles.

The kid reached the spot where the riders had appeared first. He halted, waiting for the crew to come up to him. The trail hand was somewhere below. The kid walked his horse slowly down the slope.

Cattle were pouring over the far rim, bawling in terror, a seething cloud of madness on its express journey to nowhere.

The kid stopped again. Below him one of the riders had

reined in and dismounted beside the dead trail hand. The rider turned the body over with his foot. The arms flopped outward.

Above the booming storm of the departing stampede, the kid heard a resonant, unearthly, sad voice say, "God rest your soul, my man."

It was all one vast, scrambled nightmare to the kid, as illusive as cigarette smoke. The man just below could not see the kid against the black rocks and the kid, recovering reason in time, knew that it would be madness to show himself, unarmed, to this pious murderer.

The crew came boiling over the ridge. The mysterious rider had vanished completely. Suddenly the kid realized his precarious position, himself unknown in a strange country.

Lightning spread a yellow glare across the heavens. The kid spurred into the cover of the darkness. He looked back once as the sheet lightning flared again.

The trail hand was spread out in the form of a cross, his teeth bared in a cold grin, sightless eyes staring at the chilly moon.

To find out more about *Under the Diehard Brand* and how you can obtain your copy, go to www.goldenagestories.com.

GLOSSARY

GLOSSARY

STORIES FROM THE GOLDEN AGE *reflect the words and expressions used in the 1930s and 1940s, adding unique flavor and authenticity to the tales. While a character's speech may often reflect regional origins, it also can convey attitudes common in the day. So that readers can better grasp such cultural and historical terms, uncommon words or expressions of the era, the following glossary has been provided.*

¡Abajo los renegados!: (Spanish) Down with the renegades!

Ai: used as an utterance of pity, pain, anguish, etc.

amigos míos: (Spanish) my friends.

arroyo: (chiefly in southwestern US) a small, steep-sided watercourse or gulch with a nearly flat floor, usually dry except after heavy rains.

bag of breeze: windbag; an empty, voluble, pretentious talker.

baile: (Spanish) dance.

Barbary Coast: the waterfront district of San Francisco in the nineteenth century, notorious for its cheap bars and nightclubs, prostitutes, gambling houses and high incidence of crime.

barrio: (Spanish) neighborhood.

beeves: plural of *beef,* an adult cow, steer or bull raised for its meat.

blue chip: a poker chip having a high value.

bolero: a jacket ending above or at the waistline, with or without collar, lapel and sleeves, worn open in front.

bowser: a gun.

caballero: (Spanish) gentleman.

calabozo: (Spanish) jail.

carbine: a short rifle used in the cavalry.

Castilian: a native or inhabitant of Castile, a former kingdom comprising most of Spain.

charqui: (Spanish) jerked beef; beef cut into long strips and dried in the wind and sun.

chuck: food.

cock-fight: an organized fight between two roosters, each of which is equipped with sharp metal spurs, in front of spectators who often make bets on the outcome.

cold-decked: to cheat by use of a cold deck. A *cold deck* is a deck of playing cards arranged in a preset order designed to give a specific outcome when the cards are dealt. It is switched with the deck actually being used in the game to the benefit of the player and/or dealer making the switch. The term itself refers to the fact that the new deck is often physically colder than the deck that has been in use, as the constant handling of playing cards warms them enough that a difference is often noticeable.

Colt's Army: Colt Model 1848 Percussion Army Revolver; designed by Samuel Colt (1814–1862) for the US Army's Mounted Rifles, also known as *Dragoons*, horsemen trained to fight both on foot and while mounted. The .44-caliber, six-round cylinder handgun, also referred to as a *Dragoon*, was produced between 1848 and 1860 and sold to both the military and civilians.

conchas: disks, traditionally of hammered silver and resembling shells or flowers. Conchas are used as decoration pieces on belts, harnesses, etc.

curb bits: bits used to control a horse's action by means of pressure on the reins. A curb bit consists of the actual bit with a chain or strap attached, passed under the horse's jaw.

dead to rights: to have enough proof to show that someone has done something wrong.

Derringer: a pocket-sized, short-barreled, large-caliber pistol. Named for the US gunsmith Henry Deringer (1786–1868), who designed it.

Dios mío: (Spanish) my God.

'dobe: short for adobe; a building constructed with sun-dried bricks made from clay.

don: (Spanish) Mr.; a title of respect before a man's first name.

dons: Spanish gentlemen or aristocrats.

el juez: (Spanish) the judge.

familia: (Spanish) family.

faro: a gambling game played with cards and popular in the American West of the nineteenth century. In faro, the players bet on the order in which the cards will be turned over by the dealer. The cards were kept in a dealing box to keep track of the play.

Fates: the Fates, in classical mythology, are the three goddesses Clotho, Lachesis and Atropos, who control human destiny.

filibustero: (Spanish) filibuster; this term derived from the Spanish *filibustero* for "pirate," "buccaneer" or "freebooter," individuals who attack foreign lands or interests for financial gain without authority from their own government. It applied to Anglo-American adventurers in the mid-nineteenth century who tried to take control of various Caribbean, Mexican and Central American territories by force of arms.

Franciscan: a member of a religious order founded by St. Francis in 1209. The Franciscans were dedicated to the virtues of humility and poverty.

frijoles: (Spanish) any of various beans used for food, especially any of certain kidney beans so used in Mexico and the southwestern US.

Gadsden: James Gadsden (1788–1858), who was sent by the US government to negotiate the purchase of a 29,640-square-mile strip of land, now the southern part of Arizona and New Mexico. The land was purchased in 1853 from Mexico and was intended to allow for the construction of a southern route for a transcontinental railroad.

G-men: government men; agents of the Federal Bureau of Investigation.

GN: Great Northern Railway, the tracks of which extended more than 1,700 miles from Minnesota to Washington state.

guidons: Army flags.

hoist your grubhooks: raise your hands.

holdout: playing cards hidden in a gambling game for the purpose of cheating.

hole card: (poker) a playing card dealt face down and not revealed until the showdown.

homesteaders: settlers who hold homesteads, a tract of public land granted by the US government to a settler to be developed as a farm. Following the Gadsden Purchase, the Donation Act of 1854 stated that 160 acres of land in New Mexico would be given to any male settler over twenty-one years of age, and that they had to live on the land and cultivate crops for four years.

hoss: horse.

jackboots: sturdy leather boots reaching up over the knee, worn especially by soldiers.

la hacienda de **Obañon:** (Spanish) the ranch of Obañon.

las señoritas: (Spanish) the young ladies.

lead-pipe cinch: a task or accomplishment that is so easy as to be a certainty; a sure thing.

leg-of-mutton silk sleeve: a silk sleeve that is extremely wide over the upper arm and narrow from the elbow to the wrist.

line camp: an outpost cabin, tent or dugout that serves as a base of operations where line riders are housed. *Line riders* are cowboys that follow a ranch's fences or boundaries and maintain order along the borders of a cattleman's property, such as looking after stock, etc.

longhorn: a name given the early cattle of Texas because of the enormous spread of their horns that served for attack and defense. They were not only mean, but the slightest provocation, especially with a bull, would turn them into an aggressive and dangerous enemy. They had lanky bodies and long legs built for speed. A century or so of running wild had made the longhorns tough and hardy enough to withstand blizzards, droughts, dust storms and attacks by other animals and Indians. It took a good horse with a good rider to outrun a longhorn.

Madeira: a rich, strong white or amber wine, resembling sherry.

major-domo: a man in charge of a great household, as that of a sovereign; a chief steward.

matadores: (Spanish) bullfighters; a matador was the main performer in a bullfighting event where they ultimately kill the bull.

Mejico: (Spanish) Mexico.

niños: (Spanish) boys; children.

Old Rough and Ready: nickname for Zachary Taylor (1784–1850), hero and military leader in the Mexican-American War, and later the twelfth president of the United States.

outriders: range riders; cowboys who had the duty of riding about the range and keeping a sharp lookout to spot trouble, or anything that might happen to the detriment of their employer. Outridings were inspection trips, and the outriders were commissioned to ride anywhere.

padre: (Spanish) father.

peón: (Spanish) a farm worker or unskilled laborer; day laborer.

polecat: any of various North American skunks.

Pole Star: North Star; a star that is vertical, or nearly so, to the North Pole. Because it always indicates due north for an observer anywhere on Earth, it is important for navigation.

Pony Express: a former system in the American West of carrying mail and express by relays of riders mounted on ponies, especially the system operating (1860–1861) between St. Joseph, Missouri and Sacramento, California.

pulque: (Spanish) a thick alcoholic drink made in Mexico.

puncher: a hired hand who tends cattle and performs other duties on horseback.

quirt: a riding whip with a short handle and a braided leather lash.

ramrod: a rod used for ramming down the charge in a gun that is loaded through the muzzle.

renegados: (Spanish) renegades.

riata: a long noosed rope used to catch animals.

ring in: to introduce artfully or fraudulently.

Scheherazade: the female narrator of *The Arabian Nights,* who during one thousand and one adventurous nights saved her life by entertaining her husband, the king, with stories.

señor: (Spanish) sir.

serape: a long, brightly colored woolen blanket worn as a cloak by some men from Mexico, Central America and South America.

sevens: reference to a crap game in which the player who rolls a seven on the first roll, wins.

sombrero: a Mexican style of hat that was common in the Southwest. It had a high-curved wide brim, a long, loose chin strap and the crown was dented at the top. Like cowboy hats generally, it kept off the sun and rain, fended off the branches and served as a handy bucket or cup.

spiggoty: a Spanish-speaking native of Central or South America who cannot command the English language. It is a mocking imitation of "no speaka de English."

stock: 1. a collar or a neckcloth fitting like a band around the neck. 2. livestock.

Teutonic: of, pertaining to, or characteristic of the Teutons or Germans; German. (A *Teuton* is a member of a Germanic people or tribe first mentioned in the fourth century BC.)

thirteen steps: gallows; traditionally, there are thirteen steps leading up to a gallows.

tienda: (Spanish) store.

tin-pan peddler: a merchant who traveled around in a wagon selling an array of goods such as tin pans, utensils, washboards and anything a woman could use in her household. As there was very little hard cash on the frontier, the barter system prevailed and virtually anything could be traded, as long as both parties were satisfied.

vaquero: (Spanish) a cowboy or herdsman.

vengan: (Spanish) they come.

viva: (Spanish) long live.

Walker pistol: a Colt Walker pistol, originally manufactured in 1847, named after Captain Samuel Hamilton Walker, a renowned national hero who had fought in the Texas-Mexico wars.

L. Ron Hubbard
in the Golden Age
of Pulp Fiction

*In writing an adventure story
a writer has to know that he is adventuring
for a lot of people who cannot.
The writer has to take them here and there
about the globe and show them
excitement and love and realism.
As long as that writer is living the part of an
adventurer when he is hammering
the keys, he is succeeding with his story.*

*Adventuring is a state of mind.
If you adventure through life, you have a
good chance to be a success on paper.*

*Adventure doesn't mean globe-trotting,
exactly, and it doesn't mean great deeds.
Adventuring is like art.
You have to live it to make it real.*

—*L. RON HUBBARD*

L. Ron Hubbard
and American
Pulp Fiction

BORN March 13, 1911, L. Ron Hubbard lived a life at least as expansive as the stories with which he enthralled a hundred million readers through a fifty-year career.

Originally hailing from Tilden, Nebraska, he spent his formative years in a classically rugged Montana, replete with the cowpunchers, lawmen and desperadoes who would later people his Wild West adventures. And lest anyone imagine those adventures were drawn from vicarious experience, he was not only breaking broncs at a tender age, he was also among the few whites ever admitted into Blackfoot society as a bona fide blood brother. While if only to round out an otherwise rough and tumble youth, his mother was that rarity of her time—a thoroughly educated woman—who introduced her son to the classics of Occidental literature even before his seventh birthday.

But as any dedicated L. Ron Hubbard reader will attest, his world extended far beyond Montana. In point of fact, and as the son of a United States naval officer, by the age of eighteen he had traveled over a quarter of a million miles. Included therein were three Pacific crossings to a then still mysterious Asia, where he ran with the likes of Her British Majesty's agent-in-place

L. Ron Hubbard, left, at Congressional Airport, Washington, DC, 1931, with members of George Washington University flying club.

for North China, and the last in the line of Royal Magicians from the court of Kublai Khan. For the record, L. Ron Hubbard was also among the first Westerners to gain admittance to forbidden Tibetan monasteries below Manchuria, and his photographs of China's Great Wall long graced American geography texts.

Upon his return to the United States and a hasty completion of his interrupted high school education, the young Ron Hubbard entered George Washington University. There, as fans of his aerial adventures may have heard, he earned his wings as a pioneering barnstormer at the dawn of American aviation. He also earned a place in free-flight record books for the longest sustained flight above Chicago. Moreover, as a roving reporter for *Sportsman Pilot* (featuring his first professionally penned articles), he further helped inspire a generation of pilots who would take America to world airpower.

Immediately beyond his sophomore year, Ron embarked on the first of his famed ethnological expeditions, initially to then untrammeled Caribbean shores (descriptions of which would later fill a whole series of West Indies mystery-thrillers). That the Puerto Rican interior would also figure into the future of Ron Hubbard stories was likewise no accident. For in addition to cultural studies of the island, a 1932–33

LRH expedition is rightly remembered as conducting the first complete mineralogical survey of a Puerto Rico under United States jurisdiction.

There was many another adventure along this vein: As a lifetime member of the famed Explorers Club, L. Ron Hubbard charted North Pacific waters with the first shipboard radio direction finder, and so pioneered a long-range navigation system universally employed until the late twentieth century. While not to put too fine an edge on it, he also held a rare Master Mariner's license to pilot any vessel, of any tonnage in any ocean.

Yet lest we stray too far afield, there is an LRH note at this juncture in his saga, and it reads in part:

"I started out writing for the pulps, writing the best I knew, writing for every mag on the stands, slanting as well as I could."

To which one might add: His earliest submissions date from the summer of 1934, and included tales drawn from true-to-life Asian adventures, with characters roughly modeled on British/American intelligence operatives he had known in Shanghai. His early Westerns were similarly peppered with details drawn from personal

Capt. L. Ron Hubbard in Ketchikan, Alaska, 1940, on his Alaskan Radio Experimental Expedition, the first of three voyages conducted under the Explorers Club flag.

experience. Although therein lay a first hard lesson from the often cruel world of the pulps. His first Westerns were soundly rejected as lacking the authenticity of a Max Brand yarn (a particularly frustrating comment given L. Ron Hubbard's Westerns came straight from his Montana homeland, while Max Brand was a mediocre New York poet named Frederick Schiller Faust, who turned out implausible six-shooter tales from the terrace of an Italian villa).

Nevertheless, and needless to say, L. Ron Hubbard persevered and soon earned a reputation as among the most publishable names in pulp fiction, with a ninety percent placement rate of first-draft manuscripts. He was also among the most prolific, averaging between seventy and a hundred thousand words a month. Hence the rumors that L. Ron Hubbard had redesigned a typewriter for faster keyboard action and pounded out manuscripts on a continuous roll of butcher paper to save the precious seconds it took to insert a single sheet of paper into manual typewriters of the day.

That all L. Ron Hubbard stories did not run beneath said byline is yet another aspect of pulp fiction lore. That is, as publishers periodically rejected manuscripts from top-drawer authors if only to avoid paying top dollar, L. Ron Hubbard and company just as frequently replied with submissions under various pseudonyms. In Ron's case, the

A MAN OF MANY NAMES

Between 1934 and 1950, L. Ron Hubbard authored more than fifteen million words of fiction in more than two hundred classic publications. To supply his fans and editors with stories across an array of genres and pulp titles, he adopted fifteen pseudonyms in addition to his already renowned L. Ron Hubbard byline.

Winchester Remington Colt
Lt. Jonathan Daly
Capt. Charles Gordon
Capt. L. Ron Hubbard
Bernard Hubbel
Michael Keith
Rene Lafayette
Legionnaire 148
Legionnaire 14830
Ken Martin
Scott Morgan
Lt. Scott Morgan
Kurt von Rachen
Barry Randolph
Capt. Humbert Reynolds

list included: Rene Lafayette, Captain Charles Gordon, Lt. Scott Morgan and the notorious Kurt von Rachen—supposedly on the lam for a murder rap, while hammering out two-fisted prose in Argentina. The point: While L. Ron Hubbard as Ken Martin spun stories of Southeast Asian intrigue, LRH as Barry Randolph authored tales of

L. Ron Hubbard, circa 1930, at the outset of a literary career that would finally span half a century.

romance on the Western range—which, stretching between a dozen genres is how he came to stand among the two hundred elite authors providing close to a million tales through the glory days of American Pulp Fiction.

In evidence of exactly that, by 1936 L. Ron Hubbard was literally leading pulp fiction's elite as president of New York's American Fiction Guild. Members included a veritable pulp hall of fame: Lester "Doc Savage" Dent, Walter "The Shadow" Gibson, and the legendary Dashiell Hammett—to cite but a few.

Also in evidence of just where L. Ron Hubbard stood within his first two years on the American pulp circuit: By the spring of 1937, he was ensconced in Hollywood, adopting a Caribbean thriller for Columbia Pictures, remembered today as *The Secret of Treasure Island*. Comprising fifteen thirty-minute episodes, the L. Ron Hubbard screenplay led to the most profitable matinée serial in Hollywood history. In accord with Hollywood culture, he was thereafter continually called upon

The 1937 Secret of Treasure Island, *a fifteen-episode serial adapted for the screen by L. Ron Hubbard from his novel,* Murder at Pirate Castle.

to rewrite/doctor scripts—most famously for long-time friend and fellow adventurer Clark Gable.

In the interim—and herein lies another distinctive chapter of the L. Ron Hubbard story—he continually worked to open Pulp Kingdom gates to up-and-coming authors. Or, for that matter, anyone who wished to write. It was a fairly unconventional stance, as markets were already thin and competition razor sharp. But the fact remains, it was an L. Ron Hubbard hallmark that he vehemently lobbied on behalf of young authors—regularly supplying instructional articles to trade journals, guest-lecturing to short story classes at George Washington University and Harvard, and even founding his own creative writing competition. It was established in 1940, dubbed the Golden Pen, and guaranteed winners both New York representation and publication in *Argosy*.

But it was John W. Campbell Jr.'s *Astounding Science Fiction* that finally proved the most memorable LRH vehicle. While every fan of L. Ron Hubbard's galactic epics undoubtedly knows the story, it nonetheless bears repeating: By late 1938, the pulp publishing magnate of Street & Smith was determined to revamp *Astounding Science Fiction* for broader readership. In particular, senior editorial director F. Orlin Tremaine called for stories with a stronger *human element*. When acting editor John W. Campbell balked, preferring his spaceship-driven tales, Tremaine enlisted Hubbard. Hubbard, in turn, replied with the genre's first truly *character-driven* works, wherein heroes are pitted not against bug-eyed monsters but the mystery and majesty of deep space itself—and thus was launched the Golden Age of Science Fiction.

The names alone are enough to quicken the pulse of any science fiction aficionado, including LRH friend and protégé, Robert Heinlein, Isaac Asimov, A. E. van Vogt and Ray Bradbury. Moreover, when coupled with LRH stories of fantasy, we further come to what's rightly been described as the foundation of every modern tale of horror: L. Ron Hubbard's immortal *Fear.* It was rightly proclaimed by Stephen King as one of the very few works to genuinely warrant that overworked term "classic"—as in: *"This is a classic tale of creeping, surreal menace and horror. . . . This is one of the really, really good ones."*

L. Ron Hubbard, 1948, among fellow science fiction luminaries at the World Science Fiction Convention in Toronto.

To accommodate the greater body of L. Ron Hubbard fantasies, Street & Smith inaugurated *Unknown*—a classic pulp if there ever was one, and wherein readers were soon thrilling to the likes of *Typewriter in the Sky* and *Slaves of Sleep* of which Frederik Pohl would declare: *"There are bits and pieces from Ron's work that became part of the language in ways that very few other writers managed."*

And, indeed, at J. W. Campbell Jr.'s insistence, Ron was regularly drawing on themes from the Arabian Nights and

121

so introducing readers to a world of genies, jinn, Aladdin and Sinbad—all of which, of course, continue to float through cultural mythology to this day.

At least as influential in terms of post-apocalypse stories was L. Ron Hubbard's 1940 *Final Blackout*. Generally acclaimed as the finest anti-war novel of the decade and among the ten best works of the genre ever authored—here, too, was a tale that would live on in ways few other writers imagined.

Portland, Oregon, 1943; L. Ron Hubbard, captain of the US Navy subchaser PC 815.

Hence, the later Robert Heinlein verdict: "Final Blackout *is as perfect a piece of science fiction as has ever been written.*"

Like many another who both lived and wrote American pulp adventure, the war proved a tragic end to Ron's sojourn in the pulps. He served with distinction in four theaters and was highly decorated for commanding corvettes in the North Pacific. He was also grievously wounded in combat, lost many a close friend and colleague and thus resolved to say farewell to pulp fiction and devote himself to what it had supported these many years—namely, his serious research.

But in no way was the LRH literary saga at an end, for as he wrote some thirty years later, in 1980:

"Recently there came a period when I had little to do. This was novel in a life so crammed with busy years, and I decided to amuse myself by writing a novel that was pure *science fiction."*

That work was *Battlefield Earth: A Saga of the Year 3000*. It was an immediate *New York Times* bestseller and, in fact, the first international science fiction blockbuster in decades. It was not, however, L. Ron Hubbard's magnum opus, as that distinction is generally reserved for his next and final work: The 1.2 million word *Mission Earth*.

> **Final Blackout**
> *is as perfect a piece of science fiction as has ever been written.*
>
> —Robert Heinlein

How he managed those 1.2 million words in just over twelve months is yet another piece of the L. Ron Hubbard legend. But the fact remains, he did indeed author a ten-volume *dekalogy* that lives in publishing history for the fact that each and every volume of the series was also a *New York Times* bestseller.

Moreover, as subsequent generations discovered L. Ron Hubbard through republished works and novelizations of his screenplays, the mere fact of his name on a cover signaled an international bestseller. . . . Until, to date, sales of his works exceed hundreds of millions, and he otherwise remains among the most enduring and widely read authors in literary history. Although as a final word on the tales of L. Ron Hubbard, perhaps it's enough to simply reiterate what editors told readers in the glory days of American Pulp Fiction:

He writes the way he does, brothers, because he's been there, seen it and done it!

THE STORIES FROM THE GOLDEN AGE

Your ticket to adventure starts here with the Stories from the Golden Age collection by master storyteller L. Ron Hubbard. These gripping tales are set in a kaleidoscope of exotic locales and brim with fascinating characters, including some of the most vile villains, dangerous dames and brazen heroes you'll ever get to meet.

The entire collection of over one hundred and fifty stories is being released in a series of eighty books and audiobooks. For an up-to-date listing of available titles, go to www.goldenagestories.com.

AIR ADVENTURE

Arctic Wings	*Man-Killers of the Air*
The Battling Pilot	*On Blazing Wings*
Boomerang Bomber	*Red Death Over China*
The Crate Killer	*Sabotage in the Sky*
The Dive Bomber	*Sky Birds Dare!*
Forbidden Gold	*The Sky-Crasher*
Hurtling Wings	*Trouble on His Wings*
The Lieutenant Takes the Sky	*Wings Over Ethiopia*

FAR-FLUNG ADVENTURE

SEA ADVENTURE

TALES FROM THE ORIENT

The Devil—With Wings
The Falcon Killer
Five Mex for a Million
Golden Hell
The Green God
Hurricane's Roar
Inky Odds
Orders Is Orders

Pearl Pirate
The Red Dragon
Spy Killer
Tah
The Trail of the Red Diamonds
Wind-Gone-Mad
Yellow Loot

MYSTERY

The Blow Torch Murder
Brass Keys to Murder
Calling Squad Cars!
The Carnival of Death
The Chee-Chalker
Dead Men Kill
The Death Flyer
Flame City

The Grease Spot
Killer Ape
Killer's Law
The Mad Dog Murder
Mouthpiece
Murder Afloat
The Slickers
They Killed Him Dead

127

FANTASY

SCIENCE FICTION

WESTERN

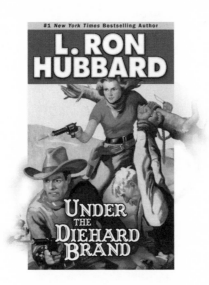